FRAMED

SCOTT STROSAHL

Everyone charged with a penal offence has the right to be presumed innocent until proved guilty according to law in a public trial.

Article 11 of the Universal
Declaration of Human Rights,
adopted by the United Nations
General Assembly, 10 Dec 1948

CHAPTER 1

Thursday, November 20, 11:15 a.m.

Everyone waited patiently as the jury filed into the room and took their seats in the outdated brown chairs. The prosecutor, Ralph Cummings, looked eagerly for some indication of what the verdict might be. Like a poker player reading his opponent, Ralph could often pick up on the little tells from the jury. A quick smile or a look of pity to either of the attorneys could give away everything. However, on this day the jurors avoided eye contact with him, which was usually a bad sign. But then again, he didn't see any of them looking at the defendants either.

It had been a relatively short trial as very few witnesses were called to testify. The only defense the court appointed attorney, Darren Williams, had presented was, "My clients don't know anything about a conspiracy" and "They are undeniably innocent." Both defendants had taken the stand and vehemently denied all charges, but neither had any explanation for the evidence presented by the prosecution.

The courtroom was packed with reporters and curious attorneys who had been following the case, and the commotion quickly calmed as the chosen twelve made their entrance. Once they were seated and as comfortable as could be under the circumstances, the room somehow found a way to get even quieter as everyone held their breath, and the judge addressed the jury.

"Have you reached a unanimous verdict?"

Several jurors nodded, and the foreman confirmed they had completed their civic duty.

"I will now read the verdict as set forth by the jury as a whole and signed as such by all twelve members." Judge Matthes paused for dramatic effect and glanced around the room, enjoying the attention. "On count one of the indictment, the charge of armed robbery, we find the defendants guilty. On counts two through thirty-one, the charges of false imprisonment, we find the defendants guilty on all counts." A low rumble progressed through the room as the crowd reacted to the verdict. "I am ordering that the defendants be held without bond and am setting this matter for sentencing two weeks from today, back here in this courtroom."

CHAPTER 2

Thursday, May 15, 10:15 p.m.
6 months before the trial

K evin Peters, a short stocky man of thirty-two, walked up the three uneven steps from the garage into the kitchen and dropped his keys on the counter. He slid his shoes past his heel and flipped them with his toes in the direction of the shoe rack by the wall. A light flickered through the doorway that told him his wife, Jenny, was watching TV in the living room.

"How was the game?" she called. Not that she cared, but the question was expected.

"Not bad." Kevin was pulling a beer out of the fridge. As he bent over, he noticed that it was an increasingly difficult task due to the extra weight around his midsection. He considered skipping the beer for one of Jenny's diet sodas, but then he remembered how awful the things tasted. He told himself that he'd cut back starting Monday. *You can't start a new routine on the weekend*, he reasoned.

"I was down almost fifty bucks at one point," he called toward the light, "but I had a couple good bluffs and ended up even for the night." He had just returned from his monthly poker game with some of the guys in the neighborhood. He searched through a drawer for the bottle opener and heard the familiar jingle that signified the nightly news was on. Retrieving the opener from its hiding place under a soup ladle, he walked into the living room and found his wife on the couch.

She was a redhead of average height with moderate good looks—not a head-turner, but not unattractive either. They had been married for nearly six months and were passed the newly-wed stage. This meant that she did not get his beer for him anymore, and he did not skip poker night to watch movies with his wife. She also didn't wear makeup around the house, but Kevin didn't mind that; he didn't feel she really needed it most of the time anyway.

He crossed the room and dropped into a worn navy leather recliner situated at the end of the brown microfiber couch. The chair had come from his apartment; the couch from hers. As he'd suspected, the Channel 12 News was in progress, and on screen he saw a young brunette standing outside a rundown house circumscribed with crime scene tape.

"We have an update on a story that Channel 12 first broke earlier this evening. This afternoon, police arrested 36-year-old Matthew Johnston of Polk City in connection with the sexual assault of an eight-year-old neighbor. We have now learned that the girl's parents reported the abuse two weeks ago when they found explicit letters written to their daughter in her bedroom."

The screen cut from the house to a stock picture of a hand-written letter, the words blurred so they were unreadable, and a photo of a young girl in a school uniform. Kevin doubted that Polk City required their students to wear uniforms, or that the picture was even of the girl in question, but a Channel 12 producer no doubt felt that it would make the cutaway more sensational.

The reporter continued, "The letters contained descriptions of various acts the perpetrator performed on the girl. It is unknown at this time whether these acts actually took place, or if they were just fantasies, but the police are erring on the side of caution and assuming the worst."

"Can you believe these people?" Kevin exclaimed in disgust, pointing at the TV with his beer. "Somebody needs to take that guy behind the woodshed, if you know what I mean."

"Yeah," Jenny nodded. "I can't believe some of the stuff going on in the world today."

"And the worst part is, now we're gonna spend tons of money to give this guy a trial, then pay for him to stay at a resort called 'prison', and after a few years he'll be back out on the street ruining another kid's life. You know, I heard a good idea on the radio this afternoon. Someone on one of those talk shows was saying we should build a big furnace. Then whenever we catch one of these perverts, we just toss 'em in. Forget the trials, forget prison. That would solve a lot of problems."

On the screen, a police officer was helping a handcuffed man in his mid-twenties duck his head to get into a patrol car. The man held his hands up, attempting to hide his face as photographers snapped photos.

"You wanna get rid of trials? What happened to 'innocent until proven guilty'?" Jenny was surprised by her husband's anger toward someone he'd never even met.

"That's a nice idea, but come on. They wouldn't have arrested him if they didn't have some good evidence."

"What if they're wrong?" she protested.

"Come on, Jen. They probably got DNA and stuff. And besides, if he didn't do it then he would have an alibi or something. I'm sure the cops checked that before they arrested him."

"We don't know anything about the guy, except that he's been arrested, and you're ready to kill him?" She shook her head. "You might feel a little differently if you were the one in cuffs."

"Yeah, well I guess I'll just have to make sure I don't get caught breaking any laws then."

Jenny threw her hands up in surrender. "Whatever. I'm going to bed. You coming?" She stood and headed for the stairs.

"Yeah, I'll be there in a minute."

Friday, May 16, 9:30 a.m.

"All available units report to a 10-90 at 206 Sixth Avenue downtown. Robbery in progress at the Midland Savings and Loan. Suspect is armed and has taken hostages…"

CHAPTER 3

Friday, May 16, 10:30 a.m.

Sergeant Max Weathers called in the next hostage and continued with the same tired questions. "What were you doing before the shooting began?"

"I was filling out one of those withdrawal deals— you know, trying to remember my account number—and then it sounded like firecrackers, or whatever, were going off behind me. Everyone started screaming and running around. It was total freakin' chaos."

The interviewee's name was Candi, a nineteen-year-old blonde who worked at a local hair salon. She sat with her legs crossed, examining her nails, clearly annoyed that they were trying to talk to her.

"Did you see the gunman?"

"Yeah, he was waving a gun around. It was kinda hard to miss him." She swung her hand through the air to demonstrate, just in case the officers didn't understand what she meant.

"But did you see what he looked like?"

"Umm... I don't know. He had a black ski mask, and I think..." She clicked her tongue as she attempted to recall his wardrobe. "Yeah, a jean jacket and black pants. Look, can I go now? 'Cause I've got a date tonight, and..."

"I'm sorry," the Sergeant interrupted, "but I'm afraid you're gonna have to wait with everybody else. As of right now, everyone that was in that bank is a suspect."

"But I just told you the gunman was a guy, so obviously I didn't do it."

"Just wait outside, ma'am."

As she was escorted into the hallway, the young Officer Riley turned to his partner and asked, "Do you think we can rule her out based on stupidity?"

"Son, you're new," Weathers replied, "so here's a tip. You'll learn someday that just because you know someone isn't guilty, that doesn't mean they're innocent. Never completely rule out anyone."

Riley thought this sounded rather ridiculous. "Well, we know I didn't do it. Does that mean you can't rule me out either?"

"Do you have an alibi?" Weathers asked with a straight face.

The rookie rolled his eyes and said, "I was on patrol with you."

The Sergeant sighed and shook his head. "Yes, but if I'm your only witness, you're screwed. I drink like a fish; I can't be trusted."

Riley thought he was joking but couldn't tell for sure. "First of all, sir, freshwater fish don't drink water, they absorb it through osmosis, so I'm assuming you mean to say that you drink like a saltwater fish. And second of all, if you can't be trusted, why are you heading up this investigation?"

"It's called seniority, son, and haven't you ever heard of an expression before? Don't be so literal."

My dad used to tell me that all the time, Riley thought. He was about to relay an amusing anecdote when Lieutenant Smith, a growly old officer whom Riley had learned to avoid whenever possible, entered the room. Smith stopped mid-stride when he saw Weathers.

"Weathers?" he spat. "Why the hell did Captain Andrews put you in charge of this investigation?"

"Because he's a senior citizen," Riley offered with a smirk.

Weathers ignored the question, "Smith, we're conducting witness interviews here. Could you go interfere with someone else's investigation?"

"I just thought you'd like to know that we checked the security cameras, but apparently the bank stopped recording a couple months ago when they ran out of blank tapes and no one ordered new ones." With that bit of wonderful news delivered, he turned and left them to finish their tedious interrogations.

In reality, Riley and Weathers had been assigned to the Midland robbery purely for political reasons. Jared Riley, a tall, muscular young man sporting a crew cut, had only been a police officer for about five months and was recently assigned to ride along with the more experienced Max Weathers. At age sixty-one, Max's well-trimmed silver hair and wrinkles were a stark contrast to his new partner. On the force for forty years, he was in decent shape for his age but would have no chance at passing the pre-employment physical anymore.

The rumor around the station was that Weathers was going to retire soon, and they wanted someone to babysit until they could get rid of him. Putting Weathers on a case like this made it easier for Captain Andrews to keep an eye on him, and the Mayor could announce that they had one of their "most experienced officers" working the case. Riley had not been a standout candidate for the police department, but he was a smart kid. More importantly, he was in the Iowa National Guard, and the new police chief felt it would be good for the department's image if he helped bring down the Midland Robber.

A heavy set female officer poked her head into the small, dark interrogation room. "Next up is a Mr. Kevin Peters."

"Send him in," Weathers replied.

Having no suspects, there were many people left to question. And there were many questions to ask. "Where's the money?" was the proverbial $64,000 question, or to be more precise, the $1.2 million question.

Kevin was led into the room and directed to a metal chair pushed back about three feet from the table. Weathers and Riley both sat in larger padded chairs behind the table in an obvious attempt to intimidate the suspect. It was a cheap trick Riley had first experienced when applying with the Des Moines Police Department. As part of the hiring process, all applicants were subjected to an interview with the board of supervisors. He had entered the interview room and saw six people waiting behind a long table. Their half of the room was stepped up about six inches higher, as if they were on a stage. He had to sit in a folding chair in the middle of the room while they scowled down at him, judging him for being small and exposed. The point of it was to see how he would react in an uncomfortable situation. Interrogators often used this technique to show who was in charge of the questioning.

Kevin tapped his fingers nervously on his leg. He didn't understand what they were waiting for. The younger guy seemed to be making notations on a pad of paper while the older one studied him intently. The room smelled like cheap perfume, and he wondered if it was from one of the officers, or from a previous interviewee. He crossed his legs, then changed his mind and uncrossed them again, wishing they would just ask their questions and get the whole thing over with.

"Mr. Peters. What were you doing before the shooting began?" Weathers finally began.

"I, um…" Kevin cleared his throat. "I was replacing some of the light fixtures in the lobby when I heard the shots."

"Replacing lights? So, do you work for the bank? I don't remember seeing you on the list of employees who were on duty today." Weathers frowned suspiciously and flipped through some papers on the table in front of him, looking for the employee list they had received from the bank manager.

"No, I work for R & T Electric. The bank hired us to upgrade the ceiling lights in the lobby—to make them more energy efficient."

Weathers paused as Riley scribbled something on his notepad. "Okay. Did you see the gunman?"

Kevin shrugged. "Yeah, we all did."

"Could you describe him for us?"

"He was about six feet, maybe 190. He had on a black shirt, jeans, and a bandana around his face."

"Six feet, 190, jeans? You just described yourself. Are you trying to tell us something?" Riley joked.

"Yeah," Kevin replied, rolling his eyes. "I held up the bank. I feel bad about it now though, so I wanna come clean. You got me."

"Alright," Weathers cut in. "So, what did you do after he started shooting?"

"He made everyone get down on the ground, and he kept yelling to look away or we would die. He grabbed me and a couple other people and took us into the vault with him…"

"Yes," Riley offered, consulting his notepad, "a Mr. Jason Russell and a Mrs. Becky Stevenson."

"Sure, if you say so," Kevin shrugged. "I was paying more attention to the gun. We didn't really get much of a chance for small talk."

"So, what happened next?" Weathers prompted.

"He told us to stand at the vault door and face out toward the lobby. We just stood there for a while, and then I heard gun shots behind us. I thought I was dead! The next thing I know the S.W.A.T. team is crashing through the door and we're rushed out into the lobby."

Weathers leaned forward in his chair, suddenly more interested in his interrogation. "So, the robber—he was in the vault when S.W.A.T. breeched the building?"

"I think so. We were standing in the doorway, but it was pretty crazy when everything went down. I can't say for sure. I'm sorry. It all happened so fast, I really don't remember much."

"Alright," Weathers nodded, "You can go wait outside with everyone else. Thanks."

Kevin began to stand and then hesitated. "So, am I gonna be able to get back to work on those lights soon?"

"Well, as of right now it's a crime scene. It might take a few days before you can get back into the bank."

"Well, can I at least get my equipment from the lobby? I've got other jobs to do."

"Talk to the officers on duty at the bank. Once your stuff has been checked, you might be able to get it back."

"Okay, I'll do that. Thanks."

Next, a tall man in his forties was escorted into the room with a young boy. The man's name was Aaron Jensen and Riley estimated his son, David, at about ten years old. Riley and Weathers introduced themselves and started in with the questions.

"What were you doing before the shooting happened?"

"We were waiting in line to cash my paycheck—yesterday was payday—and then we heard shouting," Aaron recalled. "I saw someone with a gun so we ran to the corner and tried to hide. I was worried for my son." He nodded to David sitting in the chair next to him, engrossed in some sort of handheld gaming system.

"Of course. Did you see the gunman?"

"Not very well," Aaron shook his head. "I was more concerned with getting David out of harm's way. It was a man, with some sort of mask on… and he had a pistol."

"It was a .38 revolver," David chimed in, his focus remaining on the game.

Surprised, Weathers gave David a wry smile. "A .38 revolver, huh? How do you know that?"

"'Cause I saw it," he replied indignantly, momentarily abandoning his game to look at Weathers with disgust. "It was the same gun I started with on Gangster Wars." Weathers looked to his dad for help, not understanding.

"Gangster Wars is a Playstation game he got for Christmas," Aaron explained.

"Uh huh," the aged officer said, not sure how else to respond.

"Playstation is a video game console…" Riley offered.

"I know what Playstation is," his partner snapped. "I have grandchildren for cryin' out loud."

"You start off with just a switchblade, but I hit up a convenience store where a guy was selling stolen guns, and I bought a .38 revolver from him," David insisted. "I didn't keep it for too long though 'cause I took a Desert Eagle from a druggie for payment of some debts he owed me."

"A Desert Eagle?"

"Yeah. It was much cooler lookin'," David explained. He held his hand up sideways with his thumb and forefinger extended and shot a few finger bullets at the officers.

"I'm sure it was," Weathers said and returned his focus to Aaron. "Is there anything else you can remember that might help?"

"Not really. We pretty much just hid in the corner the whole time. A couple people tried to escape when he left the lobby, but the doors had been barred shut or something. I think he took some people into the vault, but we couldn't really see it very well from where we were. Sorry."

"That's alright. Thank you for your time. You can wait outside."

As Aaron and David left the room, Weathers added, "Mr. Jensen? You might want to consider some different video games. Perhaps ones that don't teach him how to be a criminal?"

Aaron shrugged and said, "That's the game all the kids are playing right now," and he walked out the door.

They finished the rest of the questionings as quickly as they could, and by early afternoon they had determined the robber acted alone in the bank, wore something over his face, and may have been wearing jeans. Out of the thirty two witnesses, twenty didn't remember the robber's clothing at all, eight thought he was wearing jeans, three said he was wearing a jean jacket, and one swore up and down that he had on nothing denim. And as for the face covering, most agreed that they couldn't see his face, but there were reports of ski masks, bandanas, panty hose, and sun glasses. That was the trouble with eyewitness accounts; they were incredibly unreliable.

But with no surveillance footage, this was all they had to go on… nothing.

CHAPTER 4

Friday, May 16, 1:00 p.m.

R iley and Weathers returned to the bank, hoping to determine how the robber had managed to escape with just over a million in cash while the building was surrounded by police officers. The one thing that the hostages had agreed on was that the robber had last been seen going into the vault, so that seemed like a good place to start.

The vault was an H & K Securities M145, manufactured in 1886, which protected the bank's cash reserves with a layered wall system—three feet of steel rebar reinforced concrete, a four inch steel plate, and another three feet of reinforced concrete. This construction was so sturdy that when the original bank was torn down in the 1950s, the new building was rebuilt around the vault.

A fire had destroyed most of the original structure and the building had to be demolished to start from scratch; however, once the building was raised, they realized the vault was not going anywhere and decided to build a new bank around the proverbial immovable object. Although the walls were original, the door, which was the weakest part of the vault, had been upgraded over the years to keep up with burglary technology.

The original door had been state of the art at the time of its installation, with a stair-step shaped groove in the door and frame to prevent it from being pried open. However, soon after construction a new door had to be fitted when a bank in San Francisco with the special grooves had been successfully breached. The innovative robbers boiled dynamite in a pot of water and skimmed the nitroglycerin off the top. They then poured the liquid explosive into the grooves, allowing the door to be blown off. The new door had a special tapered plug that fit very tightly, not allowing any liquids through the gap.

This system worked quite well until the 1920s when the cutting torch was invented. A robber could simply create his own door in the middle of the existing one. So, a layered door was installed with a copper plate sandwiched between two steel plates. The theory was that if someone attempted to cut through the door, the copper would melt and fill the hole, solidifying as soon as the torch was removed.

This door was the only way into or out of the supposedly indestructible vault, and that led to the main lobby of the bank where all the hostages had been held. It certainly seemed that there was no way to escape the vault without being seen.

"Have you found anything?" Riley asked a technician, leaning down to place a hand on his shoulder. The man was staring intently through a magnifying glass at something on the floor and jumped, dropping it. The glass clanged on the cement, startling the other technicians in the room.

"Um, yes sir… uh… So far we have fifteen usable fingerprints and eight different shoe prints. We'll have to sort through and rule out employees. I'll let you know when we have anything."

Riley wasn't so sure that they could rule out employees yet. In fact, he was beginning to think it might be an inside job. The thief obviously knew the bank well enough to steal the money and sneak out without anyone seeing who he was. Riley imagined various movie capers carried out right there in the vault. Perhaps there was a secret exit or a group of employees had conspired together to...

"We've got video," a wiry young officer announced, walking in with a stack of VHS tapes in his arms. "Well, sort of. It's from the deli across the street. Owner says he's been having trouble with some local kids taggin' his store so he installed a camera last month. I noticed it's pointed toward the bank and thought you might be able to see through the windows."

"Good work," Weathers replied. "We'll take a look at it. Let's head back to the station, Jared. There's not much else we can do here." As Weathers left the room, the young kid looked to Riley, unsure of what to do with the tower of tapes he was balancing.

Riley smiled smugly, "Well, come on. We're gonna need those tapes. Here, let me help you carry them." He reached up, removed the video at the top of the stack, and walked out after his partner.

"Hey babe, it's me. I just wanted to let you know I'm okay and not to worry." Jenny recognized Kevin's voice immediately.

"Why? What happened?" she replied, sounding panicked.

"Didn't you see it on the news? The bank robbery?"

"Oh, you were there? I didn't know. Are you alright?" In his mind he had pictured her pacing across the living room, waiting for a call from him to calm her fears. It now sounded to him as though he had created a worried mind rather than eased one. After six months of marriage, he still found himself making incorrect assumptions about her behavior on occasion.

R & T Electric considered their employees to be "independent contractors" which meant he didn't have guaranteed work. He was having trouble finding jobs lately, so the lighting project at the bank had been a blessing. It was all he had talked about earlier in the week at dinner, and he was sure she would have remembered. Perhaps she only pretended to listen to him, as much as she accused him of doing the same.

"Yes, yes. I'm fine. I'm on my way home," he reassured her. "I'll tell you all about it when I get there."

Jenny hung up the phone and turned to the TV. A pretty brunette was standing in the street outside the police barricade recounting the events of the morning.

Around 10 a.m. the police had received a panic alarm from the Midland Savings & Loan and quickly routed two units to the front of the bank and one to the back. Other officers soon joined them as they attempted to make contact for about a half hour. When no one answered the phone, S.W.A.T. was sent in. They breeched both entrances simultaneously but had apparently found only hostages inside. Officials were not releasing any information, other than to say that an investigation was ongoing, and no arrests had been made. An elderly woman was taken from the scene by ambulance, but her condition was not known.

The screen cut to a clip of the hostages being loaded into two police vans and taken to the station for questioning. Jenny had been to the Midland Savings and Loan in the past and recalled that it was located in downtown Des Moines near the courthouse. She figured it was probably only a few blocks from the police station and knew her husband wouldn't have a long trip. Jenny saw Kevin being herded into a light blue prison van along with about ten other people, all wearing make-shift zip tie handcuffs. She was about to change the channel when she noticed a familiar face at the back of the crowd.

It was Robert Matthews, her ex-fiancé. They had dated for a few years until Jenny broke it off because she didn't feel she was ready to be married. Less than a year later, she was now married to Kevin. Looking back on it, she realized it wasn't marriage that was the problem, just marriage to Robbie. When they had first met, she was into the "bad boys" and liked to party. Robbie was a lot of fun and they hit it off right away, but she had grown up and he hadn't.

Well, for the most part anyway. Sometimes she still missed the old Jenny, but she was generally happy with the life she'd chosen.

After her and Kevin's wedding announcement had appeared in the paper, she'd received a drunken phone call from Robbie, apparently still upset about the split. She hadn't talked to him for months now though, and it was weird seeing him on the news with her husband.

She flipped off the TV and went to the kitchen to start a pot of coffee, anxious for her husband's return.

CHAPTER 5

Saturday, May 16, 1:00 p.m.

Sergeant David Shirley stepped forward, pulling his black M9 pistol from his hip, and unloaded the fifteen-round magazine in five seconds, finding his mark with nine. Standing next to him, Jared Riley discharged four rounds from his M-4 carbine, carefully placed into the target's face. As they holstered their weapons, David's brother, James, jogged across the field to assess the damage. He returned a minute later, dragging the shredded corpse which was now missing its head.

"Nice shooting, Jared," James said, tossing the dummy at Riley's feet.

"Thanks," Riley replied, inspecting his handiwork. David and James Shirley were both sergeants in the National Guard with Riley and the only real friends he'd had since graduating high school. Whenever Riley could get a Saturday off, he and 'the twins', as he called them, would do target practice at the Shirleys' grandfather's farm. They made scarecrow-type dummies out of old clothes and straw and lined them up at one end of the field.

"They teach you to go for the head in cop school?" David asked, reloading the magazine for his pistol and sliding it back into the grip. His M9 was a 9mm semi-automatic which was basically a military specification Beretta 92F. In the 1970s the 92F had been tested significantly by the Joint Services Small Arms Planning Commission and had survived being buried in sand, snow, and mud, dipped in salt water, and dropped repeatedly on concrete. Thus it became the choice of the United States military.

"Nope, they say go for center mass," Jared replied as he handed his weapon to James. A much larger and more powerful gun, the M4 carbine was a descendant of the M16 and fired 45mm cartridges at 2900 feet per second from a seven pound mass of metal.

"I see, so you just enjoy shooting people in the head then?" James teased. Jared shrugged and took a seat on a tree stump nearby. James and David proceeded to discuss which caused more damage to the lumps of straw they were aiming at—a head shot or a chest shot—and Jared decided not to interrupt them with the truth about why he liked to aim for the head.

Many years earlier, Jared's dad had been a captain on the Minneapolis Police Department. A week before Jared's first birthday, his dad was helping with a drug bust, and a dealer who was wacked out of his mind on his own dope charged at him with a knife. His dad had quickly drawn his weapon and put three shots into the guy's chest as he had been taught to do. The problem was, the dealer knew the cops were onto him, and he was wearing a vest. He kept right on running and stabbed Captain Riley three times before another officer tackled him and took the knife.

Too high to even carry on a conversation, the dealer had somehow managed to stab his dad under his vest in the stomach. Within two minutes, an ambulance was transporting him to a nearby trauma center, and the doctors were able to save his life, but not without permanent damage. The blade had sliced through the stomach and nicked his spinal cord. After several years of physical therapy, he learned how to walk again with a walker, but of course he could never return to the profession he loved. Depressed, the Rileys had moved to a small Iowa town that didn't even have a police force. Twenty years later, Jared had joined the Des Moines PD, carrying on the family tradition. In some way, it was almost as if he were finishing the work his dad had set out to do—locking away bad guys and protecting the innocent.

"So," David said, aiming his handgun at a straw-filled neon green t-shirt across the field, "how do you like bein' a cop?" Riley waited to respond as David unleashed five shots into the straw man's chest. He was more deliberate with his shots this time and didn't miss.

"It's not too bad," Riley said. "The hours aren't so good at first. They make you work all the nights and weekends and holidays. But, that's all behind me now."

David looked quizzically at Riley. "What do you mean? You've only been there a few months. You on day shift already?"

"They put me on the Midland robbery," Riley declared, only mildly attempting to disguise the pride in his voice.

James removed his eye from the scope on his M4 and squinted at Riley, confused. "Why would they do that?"

Riley pretended to be hurt. "What? You don't think I'm smart enough?"

"No comment," David said quickly.

James just smiled and returned to lining up his shot. After a few seconds he squeezed the trigger and demolished a beer can being held by one of the scarecrows. He and David high fived in celebration, and they were all suddenly thirsty themselves. Riley retrieved beers for everyone from a cooler sitting in the shade under a tree.

"So, aren't you worried about messing it up?" David asked.

"What do you mean? It's not like I'm working alone," Riley said.

"Yeah, but what happens if you arrest the wrong guy? You could really screw someone over. That's what I'd worry about."

"I saw this show the other day," James added, "about people who were let out of jail after like fifteen years because they found out they were innocent."

Riley shook his head. "Look guys, most likely that's because of bad police work. If you pay attention to what you're doing and consider every angle, the odds of putting an innocent person away are pretty low. Besides, it's not just me that has to screw up. The county attorney, the judge, the jury; they all have to believe it too."

The twins nodded. "Yeah," David said. "I suppose you're right."

James chuckled. "Oh well, it's your ass on the line anyway. Not my problem, right?"

Riley laughed. "True. I gotta admit though, it's a lot easier when you're in combat and someone is shooting at you. You don't have to worry about who's the good guy and who's the bad guy; you just shoot back."

"Amen to that," David said, raising his beer as if giving a toast. "Now, who wants to kill some more insurgents?"

No Suspects in Million Dollar Robbery

Money isn't the only thing missing in Des Moines

Police are still investigating the mysterious bank robbery that took place Friday at the Midland Savings and Loan in downtown Des Moines. Thirty-two people were held hostage for an hour and $1.2 million is missing, but Des Moines police are looking for more than just money—there is also a shortage of suspects.

A panic call was received from the silent alarm at the Midland Savings and Loan around 10 a.m. After more than a half hour of failed negotiations, the S.W.A.T. team breached the building and found only hostages inside. City officials have refused to comment, only saying that an investigation is ongoing, but a source at city hall, speaking under the condition of anonymity, has confirmed that all of the hostages are considered suspects at this point. Investigators believe the robbers disguised themselves as hostages before S.W.A.T. officers entered the building, although it is still unknown how they got the money out.

The bank released a statement today saying, "We want all our customers to know their money is safe, and we renew our commitment to security. We are doing everything we can to ensure an incident such as this does not happen again." Undoubtedly, this will help to further the recent trend of online banking, where there is little chance of being held hostage while transferring funds.

A recent study by Forbes

cont on page 8A

CHAPTER 6

Wednesday, May 21, 8:30 a.m.

fter four days of watching video from the security camera across the street and interviewing witnesses, it seemed to Riley that they had nothing. He sat at his desk, staring into his coffee as he stirred.

"We have more than you think," Weathers said to his depressed partner. He hated pessimists. They always seemed to drag everyone else down with them. "What do we know?"

Riley sighed and didn't move his eyes from the stained coffee cup. "We know someone robbed the bank, and we know that we have no idea who did it."

"That's not true. We know the robber had to be in the vault in order to get the money. We know there is only one way out of that vault, and that way out was being watched by the hostages."

Riley looked up at his partner, rolling his eyes. "Yeah, so?"

"So, the only time this robber could have left the vault without being seen was when S.W.A.T. crashed through the doors. But he wouldn't have had time to leave the bank. Therefore, we know the robber was one of the hostages, which means we know a lot. We've narrowed down our suspect pool to thirty-two people."

"Yeah, I suppose so." Riley returned to stirring his coffee. He still felt like they were far from solving anything. Even if they narrowed it down to two people, they still couldn't charge either of them. Having even two possible suspects would definitely create reasonable doubt, and that's all a good defense attorney needed.

Weathers tried a different approach. "Maybe we missed something on the tapes. I know a guy over at Drake University that's good with computers. I'll see if he can find something we didn't see." The deli's camera pointed at the bank, but it only showed the front entrance; they weren't able to see inside the building. The doors were glass, but since it had been darker inside the building than out during the robbery, the windows simply reflected back the events on the street.

From browsing the last several days of video leading up to the robbery, fifteen of the hostages had been identified making regular visits to the bank. Riley had hoped to discover someone staking out the building, but all fifteen of them had valid reasons to be there. Eleven were bank employees, three were runners from local businesses making deposits, and one was the electrician working on the lights. So, even if one of them had been checking out the bank to prepare for a robbery, there was no way to know. Riley and Weathers decided to go back to the crime scene and take a fresh look for anything they may have missed.

By the time they pulled into the bank parking lot, Riley had finished his coffee and was feeling a little more chipper. He told himself that he would not leave the bank until they found something that would point them in the right direction.

From the parking lot, it seemed like a typical bank: red brick walls, two glass doors in front, a night drop box in the wall to the right of the entrance, and an ATM to the right of that. Shards of glass from the doors were now spread across the ground just inside the entrance, a stark reminder of the chaos that had ensued when S.W.A.T. stormed the building five days earlier. A large sheet of plywood covered the openings and told passersby that the place was temporarily closed for business.

Riley entered the lobby and proceeded to the vault while Weathers stayed outside for a quick smoke. He walked around the inside of the vault and felt the taupe paint hiding the cement walls, searching for any small openings or hidden doors they may have missed. He remembered seeing a movie once where the robber walled himself in a storage room behind some shelves, waited a week, and just walked out with the money.

Riley tapped on the walls to make sure they were all real, as if he knew what a fake wall sounded like. They all seemed solid enough. He felt that it was pretty safe to say the only way out of the vault was through the door he had entered a few minutes earlier.

He abandoned the vault and progressed to the offices for a closer look. The ten offices lined the outside walls of the building, along with restrooms, a storage room, and a utility room. The lobby spanned between the main doors up front and the long tellers' counter that was nearly in the dead center of the building. Directly behind the tellers' area was the vault, with a hallway around the back to allow access to the six offices on the back wall. Many of these offices had windows someone could have potentially climbed out, but that didn't change the fact that some of the hostages would have seen the gunman leave the vault, cross the hallway, and enter the office. Besides, one of the tellers pushed the silent alarm almost immediately after the robber announced his presence, and the building had been surrounded within minutes. Riley just couldn't see how it would have been possible to escape.

The first two offices had been locked during the robbery, but he took a quick look anyway. Stepping through the first door, he noticed the room was small, maybe eight feet square. In the center of the room sat a mahogany desk, seemingly an antique. However, a quick shake confirmed Riley's suspicion that it was nothing more than a cheaply made imitation. Two green paisley patterned chairs were situated against the wall inside the door for clients to sit in. Behind the desk next to the window stood a bookcase with several financial books: Strategies for Successful Investing, Finance for Small Businesses, Investment Banking for Dummies, a few tax books; all looked new and Riley wondered if they had ever been read, or if they were just for show.

He carefully slid the bookcase away from the wall and looked behind—no hidden doors or places to hide stacks of money. He checked the desk drawers—pens, paper clips, a stapler, a bottle of aspirin, nothing that seemed like it didn't belong. Looking out the windows, he could see a neatly manicured lawn spanning about fifty feet to the parking lot, and it was obvious that anyone climbing out during the robbery would have been seen by the officers camped out there. There was a small silver maple off to the right, but not close enough to reach from the window. He looked down at the ground for footprints just to be sure; there were none.

"Jared, come check this out." It was Weathers calling to him from somewhere else in the bank. Riley left the office and glanced down the hall. The door to the utility room was open. As he strolled down the hall he glanced in the other offices, noting they were nearly identical to the first. Reaching the open door, he looked in and saw Weathers standing with his hands on his hips, staring at the open electrical panel on the back wall.

"What do ya got?" Riley asked.

"Did anyone check out this electric panel?"

Riley hesitated, "I'm not sure, why?"

"The power to the cameras comes from here," Weathers stated, never breaking his gaze from the panel.

"Yeah, so? The cameras weren't working, remember?" *Figures*, Riley thought. *They stuck me with a senile old man.*

"No," he corrected. "If you check your notes you'll see the cameras were working fine. They just didn't have any tapes to record what the cameras were picking up."

"Okay, fine. What difference does it make?"

"Look in the panel here. See all these breakers that are flipped off?"

Riley could feel his frustration beginning to materialize. He felt like he was working with a child. "The electrician turned them off so he could replace the lights. There's nothing here."

"Okay. Fine." Weathers shrugged and turned to leave. As he stepped around Riley he said nonchalantly, "So, the electrician had to turn off the cameras in order to replace the lights?" He was trying to be patient with his new partner, but the rookie just didn't seem to want to listen. That was the trouble with kids these days; they always thought they were experts and didn't have anything left to learn.

Riley was confused. "What do you mean he turned off the cameras?" He moved to the side and allowed Weathers to return to the panel.

"Well, breakers eight and eleven are off," he pointed. "Those are for the lights out in the lobby, but five and six are labeled 'vid cam' and they are flipped off too. Why would he turn off the cameras in order to fix the lights?"

"He wouldn't." Riley stepped forward next to Weathers and stared at the switches. He couldn't believe no one had thought to check which breakers were turned off. When they learned the cameras had no video, they didn't bother looking into it any further.

"You know, they weren't necessarily turned off by the electrician," he offered. "There were a number of people who had access to this room. It could have been one of the employees."

"True, but they said the cameras haven't been recording for months, correct?"

"Right..."

"So, any of the bank employees would have known that and wouldn't have bothered with turning them off."

"I suppose so," Riley hated to admit it, but the old man was right.

"You know what that means..."

"It means we just ruled out an inside job."

"Yup."

CHAPTER 7

Thursday, May 22, 7:30 a.m.

R iley came in early the next day to go over some of the video footage again. Something was bothering him. They were pretty sure the robber had posed as a hostage to escape the bank, but how had he gotten all that money out without anyone noticing? They had searched everyone of course, and more than a million dollars would be difficult to conceal. He was beginning to think maybe the money was stashed somewhere in the bank. Perhaps the thief was simply waiting for things to calm down and then he would sneak back in and retrieve it. Riley recalled another movie heist where a thief hid a stolen jewel in an air duct and then returned after being released from jail to get his loot. But where would he have stashed it? Officers had searched the entire bank several times, including the air ducts, and found nothing.

On the small TV in front of him, he watched a bus pull out of view as two police cars stopped in front of the bank. The deli's camera was mounted just inside the shop and faced out the large picture window toward the street. The bank was visible over the tops of passing cars, but every so often a large van or a bus would drive by, temporarily blocking the view. From this angle, most of the parking lot and front entrance to the bank were visible in the distance. Riley couldn't see the back or along either side of the building, where several of the office windows were located, but from where the cars were parked, he thought for sure the first officers on scene would have had a good view.

He fast forwarded through the half hour of attempted negotiations. Jagged lines crossed the screen as he saw more officers arrive and stand around trying to decide what to do. The video was in black and white, and in fast motion, all the people running around in the parking lot and climbing in and out of cars reminded him of an old Three Stooges episode. He could see one of the officers talking on a cell phone every few minutes, attempting to make contact with the hostage takers.

After a few minutes of fast forwarding, he saw a S.W.A.T. van pull into the parking lot. Several men in full riot gear climbed out the back and walked over to consult with the other officers huddled behind a couple of cars parked sideways as a sort of makeshift barricade. Riley noticed that soon after the S.W.A.T. officers arrived, the phone guy stopped making his regular calls. This must have been when they decided to take the building by force. He pushed the play button and the action returned to normal speed.

Three S.W.A.T. officers were walking along the front outside wall toward the main doors. All three carried shields and one was holding some sort of metal rod that looked sort of like a crowbar. As they neared the door, Riley noticed three more officers with shields come into the frame from the other direction. They were moving along the wall toward the front doors from the opposite side. As the two teams reached their respective sides of the door they nodded briefly to each other. The front man in each group raised his crowbar, and in unison they swung them forward, smashing the doors. Within a matter of seconds, all six disappeared into the bank.

The rest of the officers had taken up positions behind the cars, guns aimed at the entryway. For a minute or two everyone just waited. Then Riley saw one of the S.W.A.T. officers come back out of the building, say something to the men waiting outside, and reenter the bank. The officers in the parking lot holstered their weapons, and several of them stepped inside through the broken doors. Riley waited another couple of minutes, and finally he saw the hostages being led out the front doors and lined up along the building. They all had their hands behind their backs with zip ties around their wrists.

"Find anything?" Weathers asked as he walked into the room, sipping a cup of coffee.

"No," Riley replied, defeated. "There's something that's been bothering me though, and I wanted to run it by you."

"Okay," Weathers sighed. He was irritated that Riley wanted to discuss this before his morning coffee. Passing Riley, he dropped into his desk chair, set the styrofoam cup on his desk, and reached down to open the bottom drawer. Reclining, he hoisted his feet onto the make shift footrest and looked at the ceiling, clearly not intending to do any work soon.

Riley either didn't notice Weathers's disinterest, or didn't care. "So we're pretty sure the robber just pretended to be a hostage in order to escape the bank undetected."

Weathers sighed and slowly lifted his head to face Riley. "Right. I think we've established that."

"But how did he get the money out?"

"Maybe he didn't." Weathers was rubbing his temples now.

"Right, that's what I thought. Maybe he hid it and will go back to recover it later."

Weathers frowned. It always gave him a headache to think too hard right away in the morning. "So, the money has to be somewhere in the bank still?" He started to wake up a little, suddenly interested in the conversation. They both sat in silence considering the question.

Riley shook his head, "I don't see how. And I hope not, because if it turns out the money is still in the bank then even if we knew who the robber was, we would only be able to charge him with attempted robbery."

"And false imprisonment. He held all those people against their will. Don't worry. Money or not, this guy is gonna do some time."

"Assuming we can find him." Riley still thought the money was important to proving their case. Of course, they were far from worrying about proof; they didn't even have a good suspect yet.

Just then, Weathers's phone rang and he leaned to his side, reaching across the desk to answer it without moving his legs from their elevated comfort. Riley walked to his desk and flipped through a stack of papers waiting for him. These were the NCIC reports, commonly called a rap sheet, for each of the hostages in the bank. Most were fairly boring—some speeding tickets, maybe a possession charge or an OWI. A couple of people had domestic abuse or weapons charges but nothing too serious.

One poor guy had even gotten a ticket on his way home from the bank the afternoon of the robbery. *Talk about a bad day*, Riley thought. He looked at the rap sheet for Samir Zladjic, a convicted sex offender. Riley secretly hoped he was the robber so they could put him back in prison. He noticed one of the tellers had been convicted of fraud several years earlier and wondered if her boss knew about it. Even though it seemed unlikely at this point that an employee was involved, she was still near the top of their list because of her history.

Weathers hung up the phone and said, "That was the manager at the Wells Fargo out on 86th Street. You remember that bulletin we sent out to all the local banks, asking them to watch for unusual deposits or withdrawals?"

"Yeah, sure."

"Well, she says someone made a $1 million deposit about three hours after the robbery and then quickly transferred it to another bank."

Riley was no longer interested in his stack of papers. "Three hours? That would be right after we finished questioning everyone. What are the odds that's a coincidence?" Riley asked.

"It gets better. Guess whose name is on the account." Weathers grinned. He loved teasing people with information while holding back just enough to keep them interested.

"Um..." Riley thought for a moment, and then suddenly shuffled through the papers he was holding. Finding what he was looking for he guessed, "I'm gonna go with the electrician, Kevin Peters."

Weathers sat up in surprise. "Yeah. How'd you guess?"

"It's right here on his rap sheet. He got a ticket for running a red light out in Windsor Heights that afternoon." Riley held up the NCIC page as proof he was telling the truth.

"You've got to be kidding," Weathers exclaimed. "This is almost too easy. I'll call Greg downstairs with computer forensics. Maybe he can trace where that money went to." He picked up the receiver and began dialing the extension.

Riley looked back to the TV screen where the video from the deli was still playing. "Hey, did you see that?" he exclaimed, and quickly snagged the remote.

"What?" Weathers hung up the phone and walked back over to the TV. Riley hit rewind, and the picture backed up about thirty seconds. Apparently the tape had reached the end and rewound, because they now saw the bank earlier in the day, before the robbery took place. The bank doors opened, and Kevin Peters walked out carrying two large batteries, one under each arm. He crossed the parking lot and left the screen. For a little over a minute they could not see him.

Weathers was getting impatient. "What am I supposed to be looking for?"

Riley waived his hand dismissively. "Just watch, here it comes."

Weathers looked back to the screen and saw Peters returning to the picture, carrying what looked like the same two batteries. He crossed the parking lot again and disappeared back into the bank.

Riley paused the video and turned to Weathers who clearly wasn't getting it. "Don't those batteries look big enough to hold, I don't know, say $1.2 million?"

Weathers looked back at the image paused on the screen, nodding thoughtfully. "Yeah, I think if they were hollow they might be big enough. So, you're thinking he switched out the batteries for fakes that morning?"

"Maybe," Riley shrugged. "It's possible anyway."

Weathers wasn't convinced. "But he'd still have to get them out after the robbery. I don't see how..."

Riley didn't wait for him to finish and instead walked over to his desk and began to dig through another stack of papers. He found the list of items released from the bank after the robbery and handed it to Weathers. Weathers looked through the sheet and saw two industrial batteries and a portable floodlight were released to a Mr. Peters. Riley waited impatiently for his partner to acknowledge his find. Weathers couldn't believe what he was seeing.

"He just carried the money out... with our permission?"

"Yup. All of those items were checked before they were released, but no one would have thought to open up a battery; there are dangerous chemicals inside. It was checked for prints and then handed over to the owner."

"I think maybe we need to have a talk with our electrician friend."

"That's exactly what I was thinking."

CHAPTER 8

Thursday, May 22, 7:30 p.m.

Jenny was just settling in on the couch to watch some TV when she heard a sharp rap at the door. She cautiously walked across the room and stood on her tip toes to look through the oval window at the top of the door. Two men in suits waited on her front porch, and she thought they looked like either cops or the mob. She was pretty sure the mob didn't operate out of central Iowa, so she opened the door a crack.

"Can I help you?" she asked tentatively.

The older one spoke first in a polite, yet commanding tone, "Yes ma'am. Is Kevin Peters home?" Jenny guessed he was in his late fifties and thought his worn brown suit might be just as old. The other, more muscular one, looked to be in his mid twenties and was kind of cute in his traditional black suit.

"No, I'm sorry. He's away on business for a few days."

"Well ma'am, I'm Sergeant Weathers. This is Officer Riley." Jenny smiled and nodded to Riley. Weathers continued, "We're with the Des Moines Police Department, and we're investigating the bank robbery he was involved in recently. Could we come in and talk for a minute?"

"I don't know what good it would do. I don't know anything," she said, making no attempt to open the door further. Weathers stepped forward and put a hand on the door. Jenny hesitated, then stepped backward into the room, allowing them to enter. She motioned for her visitors to sit on the couch and took a seat in Kevin's recliner. It occurred to Jenny now that this was an awkward arrangement for carrying on a conversation. She and Kevin usually just sat and watched TV, so they had arranged the furniture in the best positions to see the TV. But now that she had guests who wanted to talk, she realized this wasn't going to work so well. The men sitting on the couch had to look to their side to see who they were talking to.

Oh well, she thought. *Maybe they won't stay long.*

"Have you found who robbed the bank yet?" she asked.

"No ma'am, but we're following several leads, and we have the lab going over forensics right now. We'll know more once we hear back from them," Weathers said. Jenny thought that this sounded like some sort of rehearsed script he was reading to her, as if he had said these words a hundred times before. And in fact, he had. Everyone expected cases to be solved right away. "Do you have a suspect yet?" was a common question. And recent popular cop shows had only made things worse. People watched C.S.I. and thought all police officers collected and tested their own evidence; and of course, this all happened in a matter of hours, or sometimes even minutes. Juries wanted to see graphs and charts showing hair fibers and rare dirt samples that definitively proved the defendant had committed some atrocity.

However, in the real world things weren't quite so easy. Sure, they could find hairs at a crime scene, but they might be from hundreds of different people. How were they supposed to decide which one is the suspect? And testing was a waiting game. All samples were sent to the state D.C.I. Lab (Department of Criminal Investigation), where they were processed, and a report was sent back to the local agency. A simple urine test for an OWI would routinely take four to six weeks. However, victims and the press usually expected people to be locked away within a few days.

"Sergeant Weathers thinks I did it," Riley said with a slight smile. Weathers shot him a look that the rookie was all too familiar with. Growing up, his mom had given him the look so often he had given it a nickname— "the crooked mouth".

"Ignore him," Weathers told Jenny. "He thinks he's a smartass, but if you ask me he's more of a dumbass." Jenny nodded slightly, not sure whether he expected a response or not. She got the impression that these two might not have been partners by choice. She was uncomfortable now, like a child listening to her parents fight, and wished that they would just leave.

"I'm not sure how I can help you. I wasn't there, my husband was," she said.

"Yes ma'am, but we have a couple questions about him, just to clear up a few things. It won't take long," Weathers explained. He paused, and when she didn't protest, he continued. "Why was Kevin at the bank that day?"

"He was working on the lights. He's an electrician, you know."

"Yes, and what time did he get home after the incident?"

The incident? she thought. Someone had held her husband at gunpoint and stolen more than a million dollars, and this guy was calling it an "incident".

"Around 1:45 maybe. I'm not sure."

"And were you home all afternoon?"

"Yes, I was here… alone."

"So, you didn't drive over to Windsor Heights for any reason that day?"

"No… why? What's this got to do with the bank?"

"Just clearing up a few questions that have arisen. It's probably nothing," Riley lied. In truth, it could be everything. Usually when something didn't fit, it was everything. But they had to figure out what it all meant, or it would be nothing.

Weathers continued the questions. "Ma'am, you and your husband own a red Pontiac Vibe, do you not?"

"Yes."

"And was your husband driving it that day?"

"I'm not sure. He may have been, but it's out of commission now."

"How's that?"

"I'm not sure. Kevin was going to run to the store last night and said he couldn't get it started. He is going to try to jump it when he gets back from Cedar Rapids on Saturday."

"Do you know why it was photographed running a red light in Windsor Heights at 1:23pm last Saturday?"

Jenny frowned. "No, I have no idea. Kevin would have been on his way home. He called me around one when he was leaving the station after you people questioned him. He got home about 1:45."

"It doesn't take forty-five minutes to make that trip. Didn't you wonder where he had been?"

Jenny shrugged, "He said there was traffic."

"So, you have no idea why he would drive to Windsor Heights?"

"No." She thought for a moment. "Are you sure it was him?"

"We have a picture of your car passing through the intersection, and since he was driving it…" Weathers let his sentence trail off so she could form her own conclusion. It was obvious that Kevin left the bank in downtown Des Moines, and instead of traveling about fifteen miles north on the freeway to the suburb of Ankeny where they lived, he had driven out of Des Moines to the northwest, eventually running a red light in Windsor Heights and then back east to Ankeny, making the trip closer to thirty miles. Assuming normal afternoon traffic, which was generally pretty light on the freeway, he had probably stopped for about ten minutes somewhere.

"I'm afraid I don't see how this is important," Jenny protested. It seemed as though Kevin was a suspect, and she was wondering if he would be upset with her for talking to them.

Riley sighed. "As I said ma'am, it's probably nothing. But we have to check out these things. It just seemed unusual that he would drive all the way out to Windsor Heights after the robbery." He paused, not sure how to word the next question without sounding accusatory. "Does your husband have a checking account with Wells Fargo Bank?"

"No... well, he used to, but I'm pretty sure he closed that months ago. Why?"

"Well, after the robbery we sent out a message to all the area banks, to watch for large deposits, and it seems his account is open and was temporarily quite flush that afternoon."

"That's crazy. Are you saying you think Kevin stole the money and then deposited it in a closed account he used to have? That doesn't even make any sense." She stood, indicating that they should do the same. "I think maybe you need to leave. I don't feel comfortable answering any more questions."

Weathers could see they would get nothing more out of her. "Very well, ma'am. Thank you for your time. If you think of anything else that might be pertinent, please don't hesitate to call us." He stood, set a business card on the coffee table, and walked back out the door with Riley following quickly behind. As he shut the front door, Riley smiled and nodded to Jenny. This time she did not return the gesture.

As they walked down the driveway, Weathers mumbled, "This had better work, rookie."

"Don't worry, she'll call. They always do," Riley insisted.

Reaching the street, they climbed into the car, and Weathers drove to the end of the block. They made a right turn and continued about fifty feet until they were concealed behind a wood privacy fence. Riley pulled a small black box similar to a walkie talkie from under the seat and turned the knob on top. The gadget clicked, and they heard static. He pushed a button marked 'Seek' and voices began to come from the speaker as the scanner checked different frequencies.

A woman's voice, "...to the store for milk on your way home? Just get a..."

Static... then a teenage girl, "...is sleeping with Joey, but Joey secretly has like, a major crush on..."

Static.... A man, "...seventy-five yards for a touchdown! You should have seen him. It was amaz..."

Static... Another woman, "...suspect you. They were asking about a bank account in..." Static...

"Wait," Weathers said. "Go back." Riley hit a couple buttons and they heard the woman again.

"...ought you closed out that account." It sounded like Jenny.

"I was going to, but I just never got around to it," came the reply. It was a man's voice, presumably her husband, Kevin. Riley had picked up the listening device a few years back, when he was working for a private detective while applying with the Des Moines Police Department. It wasn't exactly legal, and they wouldn't be able to use it in court, but if Kevin said anything to indicate he was involved, it would let them know they were looking in the right place.

"Well, they think you robbed the bank and deposited the money in that account." Jenny sounded upset, perhaps even accusatory.

"That's ridiculous. I haven't used it since Christmas."

"What were you doing in Windsor Heights after the robbery then?"

"I wasn't in Windsor Heights. They took me to the station for questioning, and then I came straight home. You know that."

"Kevin, don't lie to me." Jenny seemed to be getting angry. "They caught you on one of those red light cameras."

"What? That has to be some sort of mistake."

"They said they have a picture of you."

"Did they show it to you?"

"No, but…"

"Jen, they were lying. Cops do that all the time."

"I don't think they were, Kevin. Why would they do that?"

"I don't know. Probably because they don't have any suspects, and they need someone to blame. I'm sure they'll give up on me when they can't find any real evidence."

"Yeah, probably…" she didn't sound convinced.

"I'll be home Friday. We can talk more about it then."

"Okay. I love you."

"Love you too. Bye."

"Bye." Static…

"Alright, what do you got for me?" Captain Andrews asked them back at the station. He was working late and was halfway through a meatball sandwich when they had barged into his office claiming to have a legitimate suspect.

"Well, the electrician, a Mr. Kevin Peters, is looking good so far." Riley offered. "Someone cut the power to the cameras, and as far as we know he was the only one with access to the electrical panel besides employees."

"And we've ruled out an inside job, because the cameras hadn't been recording for months, so there was no reason to cut power to the cameras," Weathers added, not wanting Riley to take the credit for his discovery. "He had been to the bank several days in a row. Granted he was working on the lights, and so had a reason to be there, but he still had time to check out the building and plan the heist. And we're thinking he may have used an empty battery case to sneak out the money."

"He did what?" Andrews said, frowning.

Riley jumped back in. "After he was questioned, someone released some property to him—two commercial batteries that were supposedly used for the portable lights he had set up in the lobby. We think he may have brought in hollow battery cases and hid the money in them."

"So, you're saying we handed the money to the robber and said, 'Here you go. Have a nice day'?" Andrews asked incredulously.

"It's possible," Weathers shrugged.

Andrews sighed. "Okay, anything else?"

Riley held up a picture of a red Pontiac Vibe crossing an intersection, "We have him running a red light in Windsor Heights at 1:23 the afternoon of the robbery, right around the time that a million dollar deposit was made at Wells Fargo bank in an account opened in his name."

Andrews abandoned his meal and took the picture. He held it about three inches from his face, squinting. "You can't see the driver. He's facing toward the sun; there's too much glare on the windshield. Are we sure it's him?" Andrews asked, returning the useless picture to Riley.

"We ran the plates. The car is registered to him, and his wife says he was driving it that day. She also says he took a while to get home after he left here. Apparently, he blamed it on traffic." Riley sounded less than convinced.

"How about fingerprints? Witnesses?" Andrews looked to Riley, then Weathers, waiting.

The partners looked at each other and Weathers cleared his throat. "Well, sir. The witnesses aren't really sure of anything, and we haven't got a report back on the fingerprints yet."

"Okay…" the Captain was getting impatient, and his food was getting cold. "But you said he deposited the money in his bank account?"

"Yes," Weathers replied, happy to have some good news to relay. "It was deposited and then transferred out of the country about five minutes later."

"Okay, good." At least they had something. "And I presume we have a Wells Fargo employee who can identify him as the man that made the deposit and subsequent transfer?"

"Well…" Weathers paused and glanced at Riley, who was suddenly very interested in his shoes. The truth was they hadn't thought to go out and interview any Wells Fargo employees. They had received the call from the manager who informed them of the deposit in Kevin's name, and they just assumed he'd made the deposit. It was a stupid oversight—and they both knew it. "… no, but the account was in his name," Weathers offered weakly, knowing it wouldn't pacify Andrews.

"So? What does that prove?" the captain chuckled. "Last year I got a letter from Visa informing me my bill was three months overdue. I don't have a Visa card, never have. Someone opened an account in my name. Happens all the time. We need to know it was him. Where was the money transferred to?"

Weathers grabbed another piece of paper. This one had a list of account numbers and bank names on it. He handed it to Andrews who scanned the page, pretending to understand what he was looking at. "It went through several banks overseas," Weathers explained. "One in Düsseldorf, Germany, then on to Moscow, Shanghai, Venice, a quick stop in Cairo, and finally to a small town in the Chinese highlands I can't pronounce." He pointed to a line on the page and shook his head. "From there we lose the trail. The money just seems to disappear. We have the computer guys downstairs working on it."

The Captain didn't seem impressed. "Okay, so let me get this straight. We don't have the money. We don't have any witnesses. We have his car, which he may or may not have been driving, running a red light. Someone turned off the broken cameras in a room he and many other people had access to. We don't have fingerprints, or DNA, or really anything else that could be considered 'evidence.' Does that about sum it up?"

Riley frowned and mumbled, "Well, when you say it like that, it doesn't sound quite as impressive."

Weathers was shaking his head. "Look, boss. This is our guy. Let's pick him up and see if we can get him to talk."

"No," Andrews said. "Check with Wells Fargo out in Windsor Heights and get someone to I.D. him. Check on the fingerprint report. Find the money. Get me something we could use in court and we'll arrest him, but right now you've got nothing."

CHAPTER 9

Thursday, May 22, 9:30 p.m.

"ell, the Captain pretty much just destroyed all our hopes of making an arrest soon," Riley complained as he followed Officer Jonas Young out the station door and into the parking lot. Jonas had been on the force for about ten years and had been one of the trainers at the police academy when Riley was going through. He was one of the few colleagues Riley knew at the station and often went to for advice.

"Yeah, he's good at that," Jonas chuckled.

"Is this normal?" Riley asked.

"Is what normal?"

"You know... this... thinking you have the case wrapped up and then having it fall to pieces on you."

The two paused on the sidewalk as Jonas considered the question. "Yeah, I suppose it's normal for the big cases. There are so many unknowns, and it's easy to get tunnel vision. You focus on what you have, or think you have, and don't stop to think what you're missing. The hard part is remembering that the case has to go to a trial, and lawyers will pick all of our work apart. We have to try to think like lawyers." Jonas shuddered. "That's the part I hate."

They walked in silence the rest of the way to their cars, each of them cursing attorneys in his head. As Riley opened the door to his red Chevy Cobalt, Jonas asked, "Hey, you wanna get a drink? I was gonna stop on my way home to watch the game."

"Well, I'm not really much of a drinker," Riley started to protest and then decided he had nothing better to do, "but I guess I could have a beer."

"Great. Just follow me," Jonas said, climbing into his gray Ford pickup that was twenty years old and had nearly 200,000 miles on it. His friends were always chiding him about the age of his vehicle, but it was like part of his family, and he wasn't going to get rid of it. Normal people had dogs or cats, but Officer Young didn't have time for something that was alive, so instead he had his truck.

Riley followed the gray truck out of the parking lot and down the road four blocks, where they parked on the street in front of Slim's Irish Pub. It was a small brick building on Court Avenue that wasn't in bad shape but didn't run the risk of being mistaken for new construction either. When Riley first moved to Des Moines, he'd thought it was odd that Court Avenue, which did indeed lead to the courthouse, was lined with bars, the very places that led so many people to the courthouse on public intoxication and OWI charges. Above the door was a red hand-painted sign that said "Slim's" in large white block letters. A green four-leaf clover had been painted in place of the apostrophe, apparently to signify the Irishness of the pub. An Irish pub sounded good to Riley. He wasn't much of a "bar guy" and didn't like most hard liquor. He did, however, enjoy a beer on occasion, and an Irish pub would certainly have good beer.

Once inside, Riley was surprised to find the place semi-crowded for a Thursday night. There were several people playing pool in one corner, and at the bar a handful of people were crowded around a large TV watching the Pittsburgh Pirates battle the Chicago Cubs. The group erupted in applause as the Cubs' right fielder, Tom Goodwin, put one over the fence with two outs in the ninth inning to take the lead 3-2. Riley heard several of them talking about "breaking the curse" and laughed, shaking his head. He wished he had his Cardinals hat with him, just to cause trouble.

They took seats on a couple of stools, and the bartender greeted them, "Hey Joe. How's the crime-fightin' business?"

"Eh, you know," Jonas replied. "The usual. Takin' names and kickin' ass."

They all laughed and the bartender turned his attention to Riley. "Who's your friend?"

"This," Jonas said, motioning to Riley like Vanna White, "is the rookie they stuck with Max on the Midland Robbery."

"Oh yeah," he nodded. "Max is a good friend of mine. My name's Mickey." He extended his hand and Riley shook it. "Well, not my real name, but that's what everyone calls me," he explained, motioning to the patrons scattered around the bar. "Max's partner is always welcome here."

Riley shook his head. "I don't know that we're really 'partners' yet. I get the feeling he doesn't like me most of the time. Seems to think I'm too young to know anything."

Mickey laughed, "That's 'cause you are." Riley wasn't sure if he was joking or actually agreed with Max and was glad when he changed the subject, "So, you guys know who did it yet?"

"Yup," Riley nodded. "We're pretty sure. Just confirming some of the evidence before we make an arrest."

"That's a pretty ballsy thing, robbin' a bank during the day like that. You never know who might be carryin'." Mickey reached under the counter and retrieved a .50 caliber Desert Eagle pistol, setting it on the bar loudly. He did it for shock value, trying to get a reaction out of the young man, but Riley just nodded and said, "Nice gun. My uncle's got one like it."

Mickey smiled in approval. "Ah, a gun man. You'll fit in nicely here."

"Yup, I grew up with guns," Riley said. "My dad likes to hunt, so he taught me how to handle them, and how to respect them, when I was little." Riley removed his badge from his belt and held it up for Mickey to see. "I assume you have a permit to carry?" he joked, with his best poker face.

Mickey laughed. "As a matter of fact, I do. Although I don't need one in here. I own the property; I can have as many guns as I want."

"I suppose you're right," Riley nodded slowly. He wasn't sure if that was technically correct but didn't feel like arguing legal semantics with the man. Besides, he was off duty now; it wasn't his problem.

"Yup. So, you boys drinkin' or just here for the atmosphere?"

"If by atmosphere you mean smoke, then no, we're here for a drink," Jonas said, waving his hand in front of his face. "We'll have a couple pints of whatever you got on tap."

"Comin' right up."

They drank their beers and watched the Pirates complete their loss to the Cubs. The announcers were discussing the winning homerun by the 35-year-old leadoff hitter who had gone eight seasons with one homerun or less before knocking in the game winner. An overly excited guy in a Moises Alou jersey bought a round for everyone to celebrate, and Riley wasn't about to turn down free beer, even if it was from a Cubs fan.

After about an hour of discussing the superiority of the National League, something they could all agree on, the place started to clear out a little. Jonas caught a ride home from a couple of the Cubs fans who hadn't been drinking and left Riley to finish the half pitcher still on the table. The Cardinals were playing a late game in Houston, and Riley figured he could watch it at Slim's just as well as he could at home.

St. Louis was down 5-1 in the sixth, and Riley was considering skipping the last three innings when a woman sat down at the table next to him. He judged her to be in her late twenties, and she was tall and slender with dark curly hair. The best part though, in Riley's opinion, was the red Cardinals shirt she was wearing.

"Not a great night for us," he said in her direction.

"Yeah, it figures," she nodded, not taking her eyes off the TV. "I finally get a chance to watch a game, and they suck."

Riley laughed. "That seems to be the way it goes. My name's Jared, by the way."

She turned finally and smiled at him, and Jared Riley was hooked. "Emma. Nice to meet you."

Riley stood and moved his glass and pitcher to her table and sat down across from her. "So, Emma, what do you do that keeps you busy enough you can't watch baseball?"

"I'm a nurse over at Mercy Hospital. I work a lot of nights and weekends so..." she shrugged. "How 'bout you?"

"I'm with the Des Moines PD."

"A cop?" she smirked. "That figures."

"What's wrong with cops?" he protested.

"Nothing. Just that my sister is married to a cop, and he's a jerk."

"Well, I'm not a jerk," Riley offered with a smile, "and I'm certainly not married to your sister."

"Well, Mr. Not-a-jerk," she mocked. "What sort of crimes do you fight?" Riley noticed she was no longer watching the game. He celebrated a little victory in his head at having captured her attention, not that the game was much competition.

"Anything and everything really. Did you hear about that bank robbery last week?"

"Yeah, there was like fifty hostages or something, wasn't there?"

"Actually thirty-two, but a lot nonetheless. I'm investigating it," he bragged.

"Really?" she said, clearly interested. "I saw it on the news. I heard you have no idea who did it," she teased, pouring herself a half glass from the pitcher. Another celebration as Riley knew she was planning to stick around for at least a few more minutes.

"Well, I wouldn't say 'no idea'. It's true that we haven't made an arrest yet, but I've got some good leads," he bragged.

"I bet it was an inside job," she asserted. Riley smiled; everyone had a theory. Working on a case that was all over the news meant he could have a conversation with anybody. All he had to do was mention the Midland robbery and everybody was interested.

"Actually, we don't think so. We're looking at one of the other hostages pretty strongly though."

"Really? Who is it?" she pried.

"Sorry, I can't say."

"It's classified?" she joked.

Riley laughed, "Something like that. Just keep watching the news. I'm sure you'll know soon enough. I'll just say he was working at the bank, but he wasn't working for the bank. That should be confusing enough to keep you curious until then."

Emma relented and their attention turned back to the TV and the losing Cardinals. Riley sobered up as they watched the last couple innings of the game, and the two said their goodbyes and exchanged numbers before parting ways. Riley said he would call her over the weekend and fully intended to do so.

Lab Results Stall Arrest in Robbery Case

Police close to arrest in Midland Robbery, but lab results cause delays

Des Moines police believe they know who held the Midland Savings and Loan (and dozens of hostages) at gunpoint last week, but are unable to make an arrest until they can confirm lab results on evidence gathered at the scene. A source close to the investigation was able to confirm that an arrest is pending, but at this time all evidence is circumstantial.

Police initially had no leads relating to the largest theft in the city's history, and were considering all of the hostages as suspects. However, further investigation over the last week has revealed new information and bank employees have been subsequently removed from the suspect pool.

Fingerprint, fiber, and DNA samples collected at a crime are sent to the state DCI lab for processing. Low funding has created a staffing shortage at the lab, and a backlog of evidence has piled up, creating significant delays in the turnaround time. Departments across the state have to wait weeks for results to be returned to them.

It is a problem that recently elected Governor Kirkwood has promised to address, although the state legislature insists there is nowhere to take any money from. Kirkwood is set to meet with DCI Director George Cosson this week to discuss what options the state has and to formulate a plan to present to the state house before debate begins on this year's budget.

cont on page 4B

CHAPTER 10

Monday, May 26, 11:40 a.m.

Cindy Sheetz, manager of the Wells Fargo on 86th St in Clive, was waiting at the front door when Sergeant Weathers arrived. She was a tall, red-headed woman in her forties and a yo-yo dieter who was currently off the wagon. She was as self-conscious about her weight as the next woman but did all right on the dating scene and was not the fattest girl in her circle of friends, so it didn't bother her too much. She was twice divorced and married to her job. She told her friends it was because "that's what a woman has to do to get ahead in this world," but really she just enjoyed being unhappy. She had come to this realization a few years back and had since accepted it. The long and short of it was that she enjoyed complaining, and if things were going well, she couldn't complain.

Weathers held out his badge as he pushed through the revolving door. "Mrs. Sheetz?"

"Ms." came the reply. She forced a polite smile and shook his hand. She was disappointed to see his age. She had been dreaming all morning of greeting a strong young officer. Oh, how she enjoyed a man in uniform. Oh well. It was something else to complain about to the girls. "It's not often that we get such large deposits, but it does happen on occasion, so it didn't raise any flags at the time. But then we got your bulletin about the robbery, and we thought it might be related."

"Well, I'm glad you called us. I can't give you any details, of course, but at this point it looks like it is related," Weathers said. In fact, it may have been one of their best pieces of evidence so far, but he didn't like to give out too much information early on in an investigation.

"Wow, we saw it on the news. I can't believe he came here right afterward," she exclaimed. "Everyone here is very excited—it's like a movie or something." Weathers thought it was strange that a bank manager was excited about being involved in a bank robbery. Perhaps she would feel differently if she were the one who had been held at gunpoint and scared half to death.

"Yeah... so which tellers were working on Friday, the sixteenth?" he asked, wanting to move things along and get out of there.

"Oh, um, let's see," she suddenly remembered the papers she was carrying and consulted the top sheet. "Jamie, Kelly, and Sam were all working that day. Jamie and Sam are here today, but Kelly is off until Thursday." She motioned for him to follow as she walked quickly across the lobby, with Weathers practically jogging to catch up with her.

As they walked, he quickly glanced around the room and noticed this lobby was not unlike the one at the Midland Savings and Loan, except the offices were all in back. Entering through the front, only the lobby and teller windows were visible; to get anywhere else, one had to go down a hallway.

He saw a camera mounted to the ceiling in one corner of the room and wondered if they had tapes on which to record. They walked down a short hallway, painted the same dull tan as the lobby. The only real color in the whole place was the red stripe running along every wall at about the normal height for a chair rail. Weathers assumed this was to tie in with the Wells Fargo logo displayed on the front doors he'd just come through.

Ms. Sheetz led him into a utility room that apparently doubled as the break room. There was a small table against the back wall with a TV and a few chairs. The TV had old fashioned rabbit ears on top and large wads of aluminum foil carefully arranged on the antennae to exact maximum signal. A soap opera was playing on the TV, and he saw two young women sitting at the table eating salads from a nearby fast food restaurant. He guessed them to be about eighteen or nineteen years old.

"Jamie, Sam, this is Officer Weathers. He's here to talk to you about that bank robber that was in here the other day."

Since Riley was the junior in the partnership, he was stuck at the station going over the transcripts from their interviews while his partner was at the bank. He was hoping to find something they had missed that might support their electrician theory. He flipped through the stack of pages until he found the interview with Becky Stevenson, one of the hostages who were taken into the vault during the robbery.

Mrs. Stevenson was a benign old woman whom Riley judged to be in her late sixties, though he knew better than to ask. She wore a perpetual scowl, though most people found she was quite pleasant to be around. Riley figured it was the years of constant worrying about her nine children, twenty-four grandchildren, and seven great-grandchildren that had created the pursed lips and wrinkled forehead. Mrs. S, as she preferred to be called, had produced a small powder blue photo album from her purse to show Riley and Weathers all forty family members. Weathers had politely declined and explained they were in a hurry to finish their interviews.

Riley could tell that she was quite shaken by the incident but had calmed down fairly well by the time they spoke to her. She had apparently found the time while being detained in the lobby at the police station to reapply her lipstick and straighten up her hair, which was styled the same way it had been for the last thirty years. Riley scanned through the pages, reviewing the earlier interview with one of their most important—and least helpful—witnesses.

Weathers: So, where were you before the incident?

Stevenson: I was just leaving the bank. I was almost to the doors, and I dropped my pen as I was trying to put it back in my purse. I don't use the pens at the bank—the ones with the little chains—too many germs. I bent over to pick it up and suddenly I heard shouting, and someone grabbed my shirt collar and dragged me across the room. At first I thought maybe it was just some kid picking on an old woman, but then he started screaming at everyone about a gun. I was so scared; I didn't know what was happening.

Weathers: Did you see what the person looked like?

Stevenson: No, he was behind me, just dragging me. My blouse was pulled up under my throat choking me; I couldn't breathe. Once we got across the lobby, he finally let go and told me to stand up. I felt his gun barrel push into my back, so I just did what he said.

Weathers: That's good. That's usually the best thing you can do. So, what did he do next?

Stevenson: Then he grabbed my arm and told me to walk over to the vault, so I did. He told me to stand in the doorway with my hands on my head, facing toward the lobby.

Weathers: So, he was in the vault during this time?

Stevenson: I think so. I'm not really sure, I was crying and shaking so much... I was just really scared. I'm sorry.

Weathers: It's alright ma'am. It was a scary situation. There's nothing to be ashamed of. So, did you see the gunman leave the vault at any time?

Stevenson: No... I don't think so. I was just standing there, and then... then...

Riley: Here's some Kleenex, ma'am. Take your time.

Stevenson: I'm sorry... I was so scared; I'm still shaking... I heard gunshots and I just fainted. I'm not sure what happened after that. When I came to, there were policemen everywhere. One of them tied my hands together. I didn't understand what was happening. For a moment I thought maybe they were the robbers disguised in police uniforms. They helped me stand and led me out of the building onto a bus.

Weathers: You said "robbers", plural. Were there more than one?

Stevenson: Well, no, just one that I know of. I guess I just assumed there were probably others.

Weathers: So, you didn't ever see the gunman's face at all?

Stevenson: I don't think so. He was behind me most of the time. I'm sorry.

Weathers: Okay, was it just the two of you in the vault? You and the robber?

Stevenson: No, he drug someone else into the vault too; some man—he was standing beside me.

Weathers: Were you able to see what he looked like at all?

Stevenson: I'm not sure... short brown hair, maybe? Like I said, I was pretty scared.

Weathers: Do you think you could identify this other hostage from a group of pictures?

Stevenson: No, probably not. I didn't really see his face. I'm sorry.

Riley was hoping to find someone who could verify where Peters was during the robbery, but he wasn't having any luck. Peters did have short brown hair, but so did several other hostages, so he couldn't be sure. Mrs. Stevenson wasn't much help to them. Several of the hostages confirmed that the robber had taken some people into the vault, but there wasn't much agreement as to who these people were. Riley flipped the page to the next interview, with Mr. Toby Brandt.

Toby was a sophomore at the nearby Drake University, currently working toward his B.A. in Theatre Arts. He was an arrogant twenty-year-old who thought he was better than the rest of the people in the small Iowa town he'd grown up in and was planning to make a name for himself in Hollywood someday. So far, however, his acting experience was limited to a couple of high school plays, and a twenty second clip on "The Floppy Show", a local children's program broadcast in Des Moines. When he was four, his mom had taken him to the mall for a taping of the show, which featured a ventriloquist with a puppet named Floppy, a beagle with a red nose that beeped when kids squeezed it. Toby had been invited up front to tell Floppy a riddle, and ever since, he had dreamed of a career in acting.

> Weathers: Mr. Brandt, what were you doing before the incident began?
>
> Brandt: I had just come into the bank and was trying to figure out where I should go to open a new account.
>
> Weathers: Okay, so did you see the gunman enter the building?
>
> Brandt: No, I had my back to the door. When I heard all the commotion, I turned to

look, but he was wearing a mask, and I couldn't see his face.

Weathers: Okay, so what did you do?

Brandt: I hid. I didn't want to get shot.

Weathers: Understandable. Did you see where the gunman went once he was inside?

Brandt: Yeah, when I first turned to look, he had a hold of some old lady by the hair and was dragging her across the floor. She kept yelling and kicking. I ducked behind a large easel with a white board that was sitting over near the wall, hoping that he wouldn't notice me.

Weathers: Were you worried that he might shoot you?

Brandt: Or hit me or something. I'm going to school to be an actor, so I gotta protect my face, you know. Good acting gets you a career, but your face is what gets you through the door.

Weathers: Sure. Okay, so what did he do next?

Brandt: I think he grabbed a couple people and took them into the vault with him. Like I said, I was hiding, so I didn't see much. I thought about making a break for the door, but when I looked I saw it had been chained shut.

Weathers:	Could you see into the vault at all from where you were?
Brandt:	No. I could see the big metal door down the hall, but I couldn't see inside.
Weathers:	Okay. Did you happen to see who he took into the vault with him?
Brandt:	I think the lady he had a hold of at the beginning, but I'm not sure who else.
Weathers:	Alright. Is there anything else you think might be relevant?
Brandt:	No, not really.

Well, Riley thought. *At least we can confirm Mrs. Stevenson's story.* But, then again, he never really had any reason to doubt her anyway. She seemed so shaken by the whole ordeal that Riley felt she had to be telling the truth. He flipped through a few more interviews, but couldn't find anything to confirm Peters's version of events. On the other hand, he couldn't find anything to refute it either. He hoped Weathers was having better luck out at Wells Fargo.

"So, you were both working on Friday, the sixteenth?" Weathers asked the two girls, who were no longer interested in their show.

"Yup," Jamie said. "I was the one that took the deposit. I thought it seemed rather large, but I never dreamed it was an actual bank robber!" She had abandoned her salad and was now talking wide-eyed about the man as if she were telling her friends about a new love interest. Weathers couldn't understand everyone's fascination with criminals.

"You know," he retorted in an irritated tone, "he held thirty-two people hostage at gun point, and one woman nearly died from a heart attack."

"Yeah, but she was really old, right?" Sam chimed in. "She probably would have had that heart attack anyway."

Jamie nodded to her friend and added, "I bet he stole that money so he could win a girl's heart. There's always a girl involved. It's so romantic."

"You girls know this isn't some romance novel, right? This really happened..." Weathers couldn't believe what he was hearing. Sam rolled her eyes as if to say, "You're too old to understand." Jamie just stared off into the distance, dreaming about the misunderstood criminal. He was now anxious to leave. "So, do you remember what this Romeo looked like?"

Jamie was startled back to consciousness and took a deep breath. "No, not really. It was pretty busy that day, and we didn't know he was a bank robber at the time. I just thought he was another stupid customer."

"Do you think you would recognize him if you saw him again?" Weathers asked.

"I dunno, maybe," she said. Weathers placed a sheet of paper on the table with eight pictures on it—Kevin Peters and seven police officers that fit the same general description.

"Um… I'm not sure," Jamie said. She thought for a moment and then pointed at one of the pictures. "I think it might be this one. Is that the guy you're looking for?" Weathers circled the picture and thanked the women. As he got up to leave, Jamie added, "You know, I'd be happy to come with you to his house to make a… personal identification." She glanced at Sam and both girls giggled.

Now it was Weathers's turn to roll his eyes. "I don't think that will be necessary. I'll let you finish your lunch." He thanked them for their time and quickly exited the room.

On his way through the door, he was ambushed by the manager waiting in the hallway. She had been loitering outside the break room, not wanting to give him the opportunity to wander into any of the offices. "Ms. Sheetz," he said, recovering from the surprise. "Just the person I wanted to see. I have one more question for you. I noticed a camera in the lobby and I was wondering if we could get a copy of the video from the afternoon of the sixteenth?" She again forced a polite smile, but was clearly not happy that he was giving her more work to do.

"Of course, but it'll take a few days probably. We outsource all of our security to an independent company. They keep all the recordings off site. The camera is there to record the employees as much as the patrons. Did you know that the banking industry as a whole reported over a billion dollars in employee theft last year?"

Weathers nodded slightly, "That's interesting." He didn't really care. "Alright, well, just have them send a copy to me at the station then." He handed her a business card. "Thank you for all your help, ma'am. Have a nice day." On his way out, he called Riley for an update.

"How'd it go?" Riley asked, seeing the caller ID.

Weathers sighed. "I learned yet again how much I hate people. Remind me why I chose a career in helping people, most of which I can't stand to be around?"

Riley laughed. "Hey, next time I'll go, and you can stay here reading through pages of notes."

"Yeah, yeah. I just need some coffee... Hold on a sec," Weathers said, covering the receiver on the phone as a loud garbage truck drove by. After it passed, he continued into the parking lot toward his car and returned the phone to his ear, "Okay. Anyway, speaking of pages of notes, did you find anything?"

"Not really," Riley said. "Nothing we didn't already know. I was hoping maybe we'd missed something, but not that I can see. So, what about the bank? Did they finger Peters?"

"Nah, they picked Officer Claussen. He was helping with crowd control on Sixth Street outside the Midland building, so I doubt he deposited the money."

"I guess we're gonna have to wait for the lab results to come back then."

"Yeah, maybe we'll get lucky..." Riley could hear the ignition ding over the phone as Weathers climbed into the car. "Oh, by the way, I almost forgot. They have a camera in the lobby."

"Really? Great!" Riley paused. "Wait, tell me they have tapes..."

"Even better. It's hired out, and everything is recorded and kept off site. They're getting me a copy. The camera points toward the teller windows though and not the door, so we'll have to see. Hopefully he wasn't wearing a hat or anything."

"Well, if he's dumb enough to use an account in his own name, do you really think he's smart enough to avoid the camera?"

"Yeah, I suppose. So, we're back to waiting."

"Yup. Alright, see you back here... oh hey, wait. Did you get that e-mail from Andrews this morning?"

"E-mail?" Weathers asked. Then Riley remembered that Weathers was still refusing to use the computer. If it was absolutely necessary for him to read an electronic message, he would have someone print it off for him so he could read it on paper. Riley sighed.

"Yes, the Captain sent out an e-mail this morning about not talking to reporters."

"Not a problem. I try to avoid the piranhas at all times."

"Well, apparently someone doesn't try quite as hard. They've been talking to a reporter over at the Register. Captain wants us to make sure we all know the department's policy," Riley explained.

"I know the policy. Don't worry about it," Weathers was obviously annoyed. He told Riley he'd be back at the station in fifteen minutes, and Riley could show him the e-mail then if he really wanted to.

CHAPTER 11

Tuesday, June 10, 12:30 p.m.

Weathers pressed the buzzer next to the door and waited. Through the glass, they could see the receptionist reach across the desk and push a button to unlock the door. There was a loud click and Riley and Weathers stepped into the Polk County Attorney's office. Sitting behind a desk inside the door was a diminutive woman who controlled all traffic in and out of the office, and she immediately recognized Weathers from his many visits over the years.

"Here for a warrant?" she asked, already knowing the answer.

"Yup. Is Stan around?" Weathers replied, glancing left and right down the deserted hallway.

"Um... I think so. Why don't you go check his office? You know where it is." She nodded her head down the hall to her right, just in case he'd forgotten, and then turned to answer the ringing phone.

Riley followed Weathers down a hallway to a closed door. He was glad Weathers knew where he was going, because this was his first trip to the county attorney's office, and there were no names labeling the offices. Weathers knocked on the door and they heard a faint "come in" from the other side. They stepped into the small office and sat in the two green chairs along the wall. Behind the desk, Stan Jeffries was reclining in a black imitation leather desk chair. Stan was the deputy county attorney who usually handled warrants for them.

"Max, how you been? I thought you were retired," Stan said.

Weathers smiled, "Nope, not yet. Workin' on it though. I thought you were dead."

Stan laughed, "Almost. I'm workin' on it." He turned to Riley, "I don't believe we've met yet."

Riley stood to reach across the desk and offered his hand to Stan. "Jared Riley. I just graduated from the academy a few months ago."

Stan nodded as he shook Riley's hand and said, "Well, we're glad to have you. Sorry they stuck you with this guy." He nodded to Weathers. "Forget anything he tells you."

Weathers rolled his eyes. "Alright, alright. So anyway, we need a warrant."

"I figured as much," Stan nodded. "Who's it for?"

"Kevin Peters."

Stan's eyebrows rose. "Ah, the Midland robbery." He sat up a little in his chair, apparently interested now. "You got some new evidence?"

"Yup. Just got the fingerprint results back from the lab. It's a match," Weathers declared, as Riley handed a copy of the report across the desk.

Stan studied the page for a minute and said, "Great. So, can you go through everything we got so far for me?"

Weathers turned to Riley and nodded. They had decided on the way to the office that Riley would take the lead in laying out their case for the attorney. Weathers felt it was a good learning opportunity for the rookie.

"Well, the only fingerprint in the vault from a nonemployee was his. He had been working at the bank for several days, so he had time to learn the routine and to plan," Riley began.

"And why are we not considering employees?" Stan interjected.

"Well, someone turned off the power to the security cameras," Weathers explained, "but the cameras hadn't been working for several months. We figure an employee would have known that and would not have bothered with the cameras."

Stan nodded thoughtfully, "I suppose that makes sense. Alright, what else you got?"

Riley continued, "The money was deposited into his account at the Wells Fargo out in Windsor Heights."

"Can we confirm he made the deposit?"

"We're still waiting on the video from the lobby, but his car was caught on a red light camera in the area around the time the deposit was made. You can't tell who's driving, but his wife said he was."

"That's good, except we can't make her testify against him. And the money... have we figured out how he got it out of the bank?"

Riley and Weathers smiled at each other. "We gave it to him," Riley announced.

Stan looked confused. "What do you mean?"

Weathers shook his head. "We couldn't believe it either."

"We think he brought in empty cases that looked like the batteries he was using for his portable lighting," Riley explained. "Apparently he filled them with money. Then later, after we had questioned everyone, he went back to the bank and took the batteries."

"And you guys just gave them to him?"

"Well, they were his property, and it never occurred to anyone that they could be filled with money. Everyone just assumes that batteries are filled with whatever batteries have in them. They didn't seem relevant to the crime."

Stan just shook his head. "Alright, well it sounds like we have enough for an arrest on this guy, but we're gonna need more when we get to court. I'll get your warrant."

Two hours later, Riley and Weathers left their vehicle and walked up the short driveway to the Peters's house. Officers Garcia and Buckley were in the area and had pulled their car in behind Riley and Weathers to assist with the arrest. Extra officers weren't really necessary, but they were curious about the case and didn't have anything better to do. Weathers stopped just short of the front porch. He turned to Garcia and said, "I'll go around back. You know what to do," and disappeared around the side of the house.

Riley looked inquisitively at Garcia and Buckley. "What's he talking about?" he asked suspiciously.

Garcia just smiled. "An old trick. You'll see." He followed Buckley up the steps to the front door. Riley hesitantly stepped up onto the porch, unsure of whether or not he wanted to be a part of what was about to happen. Riley watched as Buckley removed a small black case from his pants pocket.

"Is that a lock pick set? We can't do that," Riley exclaimed in a hushed voice, not wanting to alert the occupants of the home to their presence. Buckley looked up at him, said nothing, and proceeded to unlock the door. Riley continued to protest, "We can't break into this guy's house, even if we do have a warrant."

"We're not breaking in," Garcia hissed.

"Well then what do you call it?" Riley persisted. "Unless there is probable cause to think that a crime is being committed inside, we have to knock, and then wait for him to answer the door."

Buckley was returning the small case to his pocket and addressed Riley, "Just calm down alright. He's gonna invite us in."

Riley was confused. "I don't understand. How do you know that, and even if it's true, then why do we need to pick the lock?"

Buckley just smiled and knocked on the door. Immediately they heard a man shout "come in" and Buckley and Garcia entered the house with guns drawn. Riley thought the voice sounded strangely similar to Weathers's, and suddenly he understood what had just happened. He hesitated on the porch and then decided to worry about it later and followed them through the door.

As Riley stepped into the living room, he recognized it immediately from their trip to see Mrs. Peters several weeks earlier. He noticed the furniture had been rearranged since their visit; the couch was still in the middle of the room facing the TV, but the chair had been moved closer to the wall and turned at an angle to face the couch. Garcia and Buckley had already moved on to other rooms, but Riley did a quick check of the coat closet just to be safe. He had a bad feeling about the whole situation and didn't trust them.

He understood why the officers didn't want to knock and wait. You never knew what the people inside were doing while you stood helplessly on the deck. They could be setting up to ambush you as you entered the house, or they could be destroying evidence before answering the door. There were a million reasons why a surprise assault on the house was safer and yielded more results. However, it was still illegal, and wasn't that the whole point of becoming a cop—to stop people from doing illegal things? Riley was reminded again of what his cousin had told him when he signed up for the police academy, "Cops are just a bunch of criminals with badges."

Convinced that the living room was safe, Riley moved on to the next room—a small, eat-in kitchen. Riley didn't think there were many places a person could hide, but he looked under the table and in the fridge just to be sure. As he passed through the kitchen and opened a door leading to the basement, he heard shouting from outside the house. He abandoned the basement and instead took the back door out onto the patio. He walked slowly along the edge of the house holding his 9mm in front of him, paying no attention to the hostas under his feet. As he approached the corner of the house, he could hear the voices more clearly and recognized one of them as Weathers.

"Hands on the wall!" he was ordering. Riley rounded the corner to see Weathers with his gun drawn, pointed at a woman standing against the side of the house, her face turned away from Riley. He walked around a large gray truck with "H&K Electric" stenciled on the side and trained his gun on the woman as well. Weathers holstered his weapon and approached the woman to handcuff her. As he moved her arms down behind her back, she turned her head to look at Riley. He nearly dropped his gun as he realized it was Emma, the girl he'd met at Slim's just a few days earlier. Riley had tried calling her on Saturday and Sunday, but only got the machine. He now knew why she hadn't called him back. He decided not to say anything to Weathers about it until later and instead asked him what had happened.

"I was watching the back of the house in case Peters tried to take off," he explained as he cuffed her. "I heard noises from over here and came around the corner to find her digging through the back of this truck." He led Emma to the vehicle and lowered the tailgate for her to sit on. "What the hell are you doing here, and who are you?" he demanded.

"My name is Emma Phillips. I'm a reporter with the Des Moines Register, and I was here following a lead."

"What lead?" Riley asked. She looked up at him and smiled.

"I don't have to reveal my sources," she retorted. Riley noticed that she didn't seem nearly as surprised to see him as he was to see her.

"Well you about got yourself shot," Weathers scolded. "You know we could arrest you for interfering with a police investigation... for all we know you could be in on it with him."

"So, you like Kevin Peters for the Midland robbery, huh?" she asked. Neither of the men acknowledged the question. "Come on, guys. I already know you've eliminated bank employees, and so the most likely suspect is the electrician who was working at the bank, but not for the bank." She smiled smugly at Riley as she quoted his words.

Riley was speechless and Weathers replied, "No comment. You'll have to talk to the department press liaison about that one."

Emma shrugged. "Sure. So, you wanna take these handcuffs off then?" she asked, twisting her body slightly and lifting her wrists up toward Weathers. The two officers looked at each other in bewilderment.

"Didn't you hear me? We can arrest you for interference," Weathers replied.

"Yeah, but you're not going to," Emma stated confidently.

"No? And why not?"

"Well, let's just say I'd hate for your case to be threatened by a little fourth amendment issue," she smiled. "I saw that little stunt you boys pulled."

Riley and Weathers looked to each other and both shrugged.

"Well, you know, Max," Riley said, "she didn't really interfere that much, and think of all the paperwork we'll have to fill out if we arrest her..."

"Yeah, I suppose," Weathers replied, standing Emma up and turning her around. "Alright, we're gonna let you go this time with a warning." He unlocked the cuffs. "But if you get in my way again, I will arrest you." Emma smiled and without a word returned to the street where her car was waiting.

Weathers turned to Riley, "So, where are Garcia and Buckley? Did you get Peters?"

"I'm not sure. I just got through the living room and kitchen when I heard the commotion and came out here. Let's go check." As they rounded the house and crossed the yard, Garcia and Buckley exited the front door.

"No one inside," Garcia reported. "What was going on out here?" He glanced out at the street where Emma was climbing into her car.

"Nothing," Weathers shook his head. "Don't worry about it."

The officers retreated to their respective vehicles, and Riley silently kicked himself for being so stupid. Once in the car, Weathers said, "So, give it up. What's the story?"

Riley acted surprised. "What story? I don't know what you're talking about," he lied.

"You know her," Weathers declared confidently. "I saw your face when she looked at you. And she knew stuff about the case. Since I've never talked to her..." He left the obvious accusation unspoken. Riley hesitated, considering a tactic of sticking to his guns, but then decided it was pointless.

"Alright. Last week, Jonas took me to Slim's to watch the game, and I met a girl. She said she was a nurse over at Mercy. We talked for a while and then we left... separately. That's it."

"And you told her about the case?"

"No," Riley insisted. Weathers just stared at him until he finally relented, "... nothing specific. I just said we had some suspects and might be making an arrest soon. She was interested, and I was trying to impress her. I didn't give her any details."

"Uh huh," Weathers replied, not convinced. "You know what kind of trouble you can get into by talking to the press?"

"Yeah, I know. I didn't know she was a reporter," Riley insisted. "Honest."

Weathers didn't respond, and instead notified dispatch they were returning to the station. As they pulled into the street, he mumbled something under his breath. Riley couldn't hear what he'd said but was pretty sure Weathers had just accused him of being an unintelligent person whose parents had never been married.

CHAPTER 12

Thursday, June 12, 2:00 p.m.

O fficer Riley pushed the report across the table in front of the suspect. "The only fingerprint in that vault from a nonemployee was yours. How do you explain that?" After two days of watching Peters's house, he had finally returned home from an out of town job, and they had ambushed him walking from his car to the front door. He was caught off guard and had been taken into custody with little fuss and no reporters present.

"I don't have an explanation. It must be a mistake." Kevin replied, still in shock. He was sitting in another hard metal chair behind another long table, only this time they weren't being polite. He was still wearing his work uniform and wished he could change into something more comfortable.

"No mistake. These things are pretty error proof." Error proof may have been a stretch, but recent advancements in computer algorithms had improved the accuracy significantly. In the old days, an examiner would have to manually match the fingerprints to prints that were already on file. But beginning in 1999, the computerized Integrated Automated Fingerprint Identification System— IAFIS for short—run by the FBI had fingerprints and criminal history information for nearly sixty million subjects.

"Well, I only stood in the vault doorway, and I didn't touch anything," Kevin insisted.

"Okay. Let's assume you didn't leave the print. You were working on the lighting. Is that correct?"

"Yes. The bank is replacing all of their fluorescent lights with more energy efficient bulbs."

Riley was skeptical. "Can't they replace bulbs themselves?"

Finally they were getting to some familiar territory for Peters. He sat up a little straighter and switched to electrician mode. "No, the new bulbs don't fit in the existing fixtures. All of the ballasts have to be replaced to accommodate them. It's a fairly straight forward process really."

"That sounds rather expensive for just a small savings in electricity." Riley was beginning to doubt the electrician's story. He couldn't remember now if they had checked with the bank manager about hiring Kevin. He would have to consult his notes to be sure. He had a problem with automatically trusting what people told him. It was an issue he was working to overcome. For some reason he felt bad when he doubted people for no reason. Even if they didn't know that he didn't believe them, he felt like they could somehow tell he thought they were lying. And he definitely didn't like letting other people know what he was thinking. Weathers, on the other hand, was skeptical of everything, trusted no one, and had no interest in "working to overcome it".

"It is expensive," Kevin said, nodding. "The savings on their electric bill won't offset the cost of replacing all the lights in the building." Riley waited a few seconds for an explanation, but it seemed Peters needed some prompting.

"So, then why would they do it?"

"The government is giving rebates to help cover the costs of installation through the end of the year. You know, to help with global warming and whatnot." He motioned to the ceiling. "You know, you guys really ought to do the lights here in the station while the government will still pay for it."

"Right... you know we are the government, don't you?" Riley said, frowning at the man's apparent ignorance.

Kevin shrugged. "Whatever. Just tryin' to help."

"Yeah, thanks. So anyway, back to the Midland Building. I assume you had to cut the power to the lights before you changed out the fixtures?"

"Sure. Safety first, you know."

"So, you had access to the electrical panel in the utility room?"

"Yeah, so what?" Kevin was slowly shrinking back down into his chair again.

"Someone cut the power to the cameras. You had the tools and access to the box." Riley was on the attack.

"Everyone that worked there had access," Kevin protested. "The room wasn't locked."

"But the cameras didn't work. An employee would have known that and wouldn't have wasted time cutting the power."

"Look, I didn't cut any wires." Kevin was starting to get upset. "I flipped a breaker for the lights at the east end of the lobby. That's it."

"Okay, then how do you explain the one million dollars deposited in Wells Fargo account number 5726-346. That is your account, isn't it?"

Kevin shifted his weight in the chair, apparently not expecting this. He opened his mouth, but no words came out.

"Well?" Riley pushed. "Is it or isn't it?"

"I... I'm not sure," Kevin managed. "I don't know my account number. I haven't used my Wells Fargo account for months."

"Well, we checked, and according to their records, that account belongs to you, and someone deposited a million dollars the afternoon of the robbery and then a few minutes later, transferred it to a bank in Dusseldorf, Germany."

"Hold on a minute!" Kevin exclaimed. "I've never even been to Germany."

"Well, the money didn't stay in Germany long. So far we've tracked it through Moscow, Shanghai, Venice, Cairo, and the Chinese Highlands. That's where we get stuck. But don't worry, we're working on it, and we'll find out where you sent that money."

Kevin's eyes were wide now, and he leaned forward on the table as he spoke with a new intensity in his voice. "I didn't send any money anywhere. This is ridiculous. It's like I'm having some sort of bad dream." He was beginning to sweat, and his breathing quickened. Riley thought he might hyperventilate, but then this was all an act of course. He was obviously lying and good at it too. Riley decided to cut to the chase.

"So, motive is easy: money. You obviously had means and opportunity. You had access to the electrical box for the cameras. You admit to being in the bank, and the vault, during the robbery. Add that to the fingerprint and the money being deposited into your account, and we've got a slam-dunk case.

"So, here's the deal. There was another two hundred grand stolen from that bank that didn't make it into your account. Now, my partner here thinks you blew it on strippers and drugs," Riley nodded toward Weathers, lurking in the corner with his arms crossed, studying Kevin's every move. "But I figure you probably had help and had to pay off your accomplices. You sign a full confession right now including their names, return the money, and maybe we'll talk to the DA and try to get you some leniency at sentencing. We already have your verbal confession anyway."

"Confession? What confession? I haven't admitted to anything." The confused look was back.

"Sure you did. It's right here in my notes." Riley pulled out a blue notepad and flipped through the pages. "Here it is. When we interviewed you after the robbery, I asked, 'Did you see the gunman?' You replied, 'Yeah, he was about six feet, maybe 190. He had on a black shirt, jeans, and a bandana around his face.' I asked, 'You just described yourself. Are you trying to tell us something?' You said, 'Yeah, I held up the bank. I feel bad about it now though, so I wanna come clean.'" He snapped the notepad shut and crossed his arms with a satisfied smirk on his face.

Kevin couldn't believe what he was hearing. "This is ridiculous," he laughed nervously as if they might be pulling his leg. "You're taking that whole thing out of context. I was being sarcastic."

"The jury won't see it that way," Weathers smiled.

"What? What jury? I didn't do anything. You've got this all wrong. I told you, I didn't cut any wires. I didn't deposit any money. I was just replacing some lights. This is crazy. Besides, how much money was missing, a million dollars? You think I just had that stuffed in my pockets while you were questioning me?"

Riley nodded and shook his finger at Peters. "Yeah, that one had us stumped for a while. We have video of you swapping out the batteries before the robbery." Riley smiled smugly, the victor in a battle of wits.

Kevin looked from Riley to Weathers and back, trying to grasp what they were getting at. "So? When I showed up that morning, the batteries for my portable lights were dead, so I brought in new ones from my truck. What does that have to do with the money?"

"It's no use lying about it. We found the empty battery cases at your house. Pretty clever, I have to say. From the outside I couldn't tell at all. Looked just like a normal battery."

"You found what?" Kevin exclaimed.

Riley ignored the question. "If you don't play ball, the DA will be asking for the maximum at sentencing when you're convicted. And you will be convicted, I guarantee that. You're best chance at seeing daylight again is to sign a full confession right now."

"I won't confess, because I didn't do anything." Kevin held up his hands dismissively.

"Alright. Fine. We've got enough to charge you. We just thought you'd like to avoid the hassle of a trial." Riley left the room, and two other officers entered. One was a short stocky man who most likely had difficulty meeting the physical fitness standards for the department. The other, however, looked like he could be a linebacker. He was about 6'6" and could probably tear Kevin's arms off if he wanted to.

They ordered Kevin to stand and escorted him to the booking room. He followed the officers down a long hallway to an open door and entered a small room with a counter along the side wall and two hard plastic chairs in one corner. They sat him in one of the chairs while they prepared for fingerprinting. Kevin continued to plead his case to these officers, but they didn't want to hear it.

"You can't do this. You've got the wrong guy," he argued. They were ignoring his entreaties, and he could feel panic building inside. It seemed like the walls were closing in on him, and he instinctively stood up.

"Sit down," the big guy ordered.

"I need some air... I... I can't breathe," Kevin gasped. He crossed the room and headed for the door.

"I said stay in that chair!" The stocky guy grabbed Kevin's arms and started to push him back down into the seat. Kevin twisted away from him and continued toward the door. He could only concentrate on one thing— getting out of that room.

He was about to step into the hall when the bigger guy threw his arm across Kevin's chest while sweeping his leg across the back of his ankles. Kevin's legs flew into the air and he crashed to the ground, landing on his back with a loud thump. He was dazed momentarily and moaned slightly as the officers rolled him over and cuffed his hands behind his back. The big guy lifted him up roughly and set him back in the chair while the stocky one grabbed another set of handcuffs and hooked his ankles to the chair leg.

They waited a few minutes, allowing him to calm down and were eventually able to complete the booking process without further incident.

CHAPTER 13

Thursday, June 12, 5:00 p.m.

Riley was shutting down his computer so he could head home for the day when he noticed his partner in Captain Andrews's office. Suddenly, their conversation from earlier in the week popped into his mind, and he began to worry that Weathers was spilling the beans to the boss. He decided to stick around and see what happened. A few minutes later, Weathers exited the office and left the building without acknowledging Riley's presence.

Riley knocked on the Captain's door and then entered after a wave through the window. He had answered the phone and was saying something about picking up groceries after work; Riley assumed it was Mrs. Andrews. He stood in the doorway as he waited for the call to end.

"Jared, just the man I wanted to talk to," Andrews said as he dropped his phone on the desk.

"Yes, sir?"

"I just wanted to make sure you're clear on our policy about the press."

Riley silently cursed Weathers. *Stupid old man.* "Yes, sir. I'm clear. And I got the e-mail earlier this week as well."

"Well, there is a reporter over at the Register who seems to know an awful lot about our investigation, and the Mayor has asked me to speak with all of our officers. I just got done talking to Max," Andrews paused, waiting for a reaction from Riley. He had learned many years earlier that the best way to get someone to talk is to leave awkward silences in the conversation. Most people will say anything to avoid silence.

"Sir, if I may," Riley interjected. "Max and I have not been together long, and I'm not sure that the chemistry is really there. In fact, I don't think he likes me sometimes. And whatever he told you about me and the press is a lie..."

"Really?" Andrews interrupted with raised eyebrows. "So, when he told me that you were a good kid and a solid cop, and there was no way you were talking to anyone, he was lying?"

Riley was surprised and momentarily speechless, but quickly regained his composure. "Um... no, sir. That's the truth." He couldn't believe how stupid he was being. His partner had covered for him, and then he had almost let the cat out of the bag himself.

Andrews eyed him suspiciously. "Is there anything else you'd like to add on the topic, son?"

"No, sir. That's about it." Riley was quickly learning the benefits of being brief.

"Alright, well just remember, talk to no one. Personally, I'm more concerned with catching the bad guys than worrying about the public image, but I've got people breathing down my neck on this case, so stay on your toes."

"Yes, of course, sir. I will." Riley retreated back to his desk and left the station before he could get himself in any more trouble.

Built directly across the street from the courthouse downtown, the jail was within sight of the Midland Savings and Loan. As Jenny parked her car, she felt strange seeing the bank again after all that had happened in the preceding weeks. The bank had a hand drawn sign on the door notifying passersby that they were indeed open once again. This was necessary because the plywood still covered the doors, and the building had a vague condemned feel to it. She stood on the sidewalk for a moment and studied the bank, wondering if the police had any idea what really happened in there that day.

Crossing the street, Jenny pushed open the large glass doors and stepped into the Polk County Jail. She had never been in a jail before and wasn't really sure what to expect. Once inside, she could see that there was a waiting area of sorts, with a couple of benches along one wall. On the opposite wall was a window with a speaker in the middle of it, not unlike a ticket window. She suddenly had a flashback to a month earlier when she had bought Iowa Cubs tickets down the street at Sec Taylor Stadium.

Jenny approached the window and saw a woman filling out some paperwork on the other side. From her uniform, Jenny learned see she was a Polk County Sherriff's Deputy.

A distorted voice came from the speaker, "Can I help you?"

"Yes," Jenny replied. "I need to know how to bond someone out."

"Name?"

"Kevin Peters." The deputy typed the name into a computer.

"Okay, it looks like he's still being booked in right now, but you can go ahead and post bond if you'd like. Let me just check on the amount here…" Now she was clicking the mouse, "looks like it's gonna be two hundred grand."

"200,000!" Jenny exclaimed. "I don't have that kind of money."

The deputy showed no signs of compassion. "Well, you could use a bondsman if you'd like. There's a list on the wall to your right." She returned to her paperwork, apparently done with the conversation. Jenny looked at a sheet of paper taped to the wall beside the window and saw a list of names and phone numbers. She typed the first number into her cell phone and hit send. It rang ten times, and she finally hung up. This continued for the next five numbers until she found some success with lucky number seven.

"Hello, Midwest Bailbonds," a man answered.

"Yes, I wanted to find out about bonding someone out of jail."

"Okay, what's the name?"

"Kevin Peters." She could hear distant typing as he looked the name up on the jail's website.

"Okay, looks like his bond is $200,000, which means you'll need to post twenty."

"20,000?"

"Yep. Ten percent."

"But then I get that back when he shows up for court, right?"

"Nope. We keep that as our fee."

"But I don't have $20,000."

"Then I guess he stays in jail. Sorry ma'am, that's the way this works." She muttered a weak "thanks" and hung up. From behind the window the deputy asked which bondsmen she was going to use. Jenny looked back to the window. The paperwork was gone, apparently finished, and now the deputy needed something to do and was interested in her again.

"I'm not sure," Jenny replied, staring at the list on the wall. "I just called Midwest Bailbonds, and they said it will cost me $20,000!"

"Yup, ten percent," the deputy nodded. "They put up the $20,000 and promise to pay the rest if he doesn't show up for court. Since they are taking the risk of losing $180,000, they keep the 20,000 as a fee."

"But who has $20,000?"

"Not many people. A bond that high, they usually don't get out."

"So, he just has to sit in jail?"

The deputy shrugged, "Yeah, but he'll get credit for it when he gets convicted."

"You mean if he gets convicted," Jenny corrected.

The deputy laughed. "Yeah, sure... *if* he gets convicted."

"Well, can I at least see him then?"

"Umm…" the deputy was typing on the computer again. "Yeah, that should be okay. He's done with booking now. As long as he put you on his visitor list. What is your name?"

"Jenny Peters. I'm his wife."

"Okay, let me go check." She disappeared around a corner. While she was waiting, Jenny wandered around the room and noticed a large map on one wall. She investigated further and found it was a map of convicted sex offenders in the area. She was amazed at the number of red dots all over town, and was thinking that maybe she should move, but then decided it was probably the same way everywhere else too.

"Ma'am?" she heard the distorted voice say from the window speaker. She crossed the room and saw the deputy was back.

"He hasn't filled out a request to allow you to visit, so you'll have to come back another time. Sorry."

"But, I'm his wife. Why wouldn't he want me to visit?"

"Sorry, but those are the rules. Unless he fills out a visitor request for you, you can't visit, no matter who you are."

Jenny offered a curt thanks and left the jail defeated, with no plan to bring her husband home any time soon.

$200,000 Bond for Midland Robber

District Court Judge sets bond at only a sixth of the amount stolen from bank

It took nearly four weeks, but detectives with the Des Moines Police Department finally made an arrest yesterday related to the largest bank robbery in the city's history.

On May 19th, dozens of people were held captive at the Midland Savings and Loan as a masked man took more than $1 million before escaping undetected. According to Captain Andrews with the Des Moines Investigative Unit, we now know who that man was.

Kevin Peters, 33, of Ankeny, was arrested Thursday after an exhaustive investigation spanning the course of several weeks. Peters, who works for R & T Electric, was originally thought to be one of the hostages, but members of the Police Cybercrimes Unit have tracked the money to an account owned by the electrician. This discovery, combined with physical evidence recovered at the scene, was enough for an arrest warrant.

Sources close to the investigation indicate that there is video of Peters carrying the money out of the bank, and he may even have confessed during questioning subsequent to his arrest.

He is charged with armed robbery and thirty-one counts of false imprisonment and is being held on $200,000 bond. Unless Peters posts bond, he will remain in the Polk County Jail awaiting his arraignment next week.

It is shaping up to be a busy month for the Polk County Attorney, as they are also scheduled to start the trial for accused child molester Matthew Johnston on Monday, a trial that is expected to last several weeks. The County Attorney

cont on page 13D

CHAPTER 14

Friday, June 13, 8:30 a.m.

T he next morning, Kevin awoke slowly. He hadn't slept well. The bed was hard and lumpy, and he'd never been in jail before; he was anxious about the possibility of an extended stay. After a bland breakfast, he was handcuffed and herded with about twenty other inmates down a series of halls to a small courtroom. To save the time and expense of transporting inmates to the courthouse, not to mention the security issues involved, Polk County had a judge that held hearings in the jail for anyone currently in custody. Kevin followed the orange jump suit in front of him and took a seat along the wall.

As they waited, Kevin surveyed the room. It seemed small for a courtroom, but he wasn't really sure how big a courtroom was supposed to be, since he had never been in one before. There was a tall wooden desk of sorts in one corner, which he guessed to be the judge's bench. In the center of the room was a long table where several men in suits sat, chatting casually. Kevin assumed these were probably lawyers. The only other furniture in the room was a row of chairs along one wall where Kevin was currently waiting. There was no jury box since the county didn't hold trials at the jail. He noticed a camera mounted on the Judge's bench pointing out into the room. This feed was routed to a TV in the "viewing area" next to the lobby inside the main entrance. Visitors were not allowed in the courtroom, since it was inside the secure section of the jail, and had to watch the proceedings on a monitor.

A woman emerged from a back room somewhere and began calling out names from a clipboard, "Jeff Barnes, Rodney Frost, Kevin Peters, Allen Duke, Carlos Rosales." Kevin raised his hand the best he could with the handcuffs on. The petite woman walked slowly across the room to the line of chairs. As Kevin watched her talk with one of the other prisoners, he could tell she had no desire to be at work today. He also noticed her puffy eyes and thought she might be hung over.

She repeated the same question to everyone, "Are you going to hire a lawyer or represent yourself?" Kevin wasn't sure; he hadn't even known he needed a lawyer until less than twenty-four hours earlier. Jeff Barnes and Allen Duke said they would represent themselves and were each given a form to sign waiving their rights to an attorney. Rodney Frost said he already had an attorney and pointed at one of the tables where four men in suits were laughing about something. When she got to Carlos Rosales he simply said, "No entiendo que."

She repeated her question louder this time, as if that would somehow make him comprehend the language better, "Are you going to hire a lawyer or represent yourself?"

Carlos said, "Lo siento. No hablo Inglés."

She looked at him with a blank stare, obviously not understanding.

Kevin had picked up some Spanish a few years earlier while working for Capital City Electric. They generally had four or five illegal aliens from various countries to the south (which of course the company affectionately called "undocumented workers") working on their crew at any one time. He turned to the woman and said, "He said he doesn't speak English."

Surprised, she turned to Kevin and said, "Oh. Well, tell him that he'll have to wait for an interpreter then. She probably won't be here for about an hour."

Kevin did his best to translate, "Traductor vendrá. Una hora." (Translator will come. One hour.) He held up one finger, hoping to help him understand.

The man nodded that he got the message and said, "Gracias."

The woman moved on to Kevin. "Are you going to hire a lawyer or represent yourself?" She was beginning to sound like a broken record.

Kevin said, "I don't know. I think I need to get an attorney, but I don't think I can afford one."

She sighed. "Do you wanna apply for the Public Defender?" she asked impatiently. She didn't seem to be much of a people person.

"Sure, I suppose," he shrugged. She dropped an application form and a pen in his lap and disappeared into another room. Kevin got the feeling that she expected him to know how the whole process worked, but he'd never been arrested before. He filled in his name, address, employer, salary, etc. and then waited, unsure of what to do next.

Eventually she returned and took the paper from him. "Okay, just wait for the judge to call you up."

Kevin sat in the uncomfortable chair wishing he knew what was going on. He had just been arrested the previous day, and already he was going to see a judge? Maybe this was good. Maybe he could get the judge to listen to him and understand that he was innocent and wasn't supposed to be there. Nobody else seemed to.

Kevin saw a woman in her mid fifties walk into the room wearing a black robe, presumably the judge. He started to stand up and then realized no one else was following suit. He quickly sat back down, not wanting to stand out. She strolled up to the bench and took her seat, apparently not concerned that people didn't "all rise." Kevin was quickly learning that real-life court didn't happen the way he'd seen on TV.

The nameplate on the judge's bench read "Hon. Jean Matthes". She had been a judge for nearly ten years and was reasonably well liked by most of the attorneys. She was regarded as tough but fair by both sides, and most days, felt she was somehow making the world a better place. Before her appointment to the bench, she had worked at a small firm in Des Moines for eighteen years doing mostly civil work and had jumped at the chance to work in the criminal system.

As Kevin waited in the hard chair, the judge invited up one defendant after another until finally his name was called. He stood and walked up in front of the judge's bench as he had seen everyone before him do. She said, "This is the date and time set for initial appearance. I've appointed the public defender to represent you. I'm entering a plea of not guilty and continuing your bond. I've set an arraignment date of July 17th at 8:00 a.m. over in the Polk County Courthouse and an in-custody arraignment date next Wednesday at 1:30 p.m. here in Jail Court. Step to the side and the court attendant will get you your copies. Your lawyer will call you up to speak with you in a minute." Kevin just stood there in shock. He was surprised at how quickly the whole event had gone. He hadn't had a chance to explain to the judge that he wasn't even supposed to be here.

"Excuse me, your honor. There's been some mistake," he said finally. "I didn't rob that bank, and I shouldn't be in here."

Judge Matthes studied him for a minute, then turned to all the other men sitting along the wall. "How many of you are innocent and think I should just dismiss your case?" Kevin heard chuckling and glanced back to see most of the men sitting along the wall had their hands raised. Under different circumstances, this may have been a humorous situation. Twenty men in orange jumpsuits, many of them hung-over and a few still high or drunk, were raising their hands—raising both their hands together since they were all still wearing handcuffs.

Kevin turned back to the judge. "No, but you don't understand. I really am innocent."

"Well, then I expect you'll be taking this to trial. Talk to your lawyer about it." She grabbed the next file and called out the name, indicating she was done with him.

Kevin walked over to his right where the woman who had called his name before handed him a sheet of paper. She told him to have a seat and that someone would call him up in a few minutes. He sat back down and looked over the paper she had given him.

IN THE IOWA DISTRICT COURT IN AND FOR POLK COUNTY

STATE OF IOWA,
   Plaintiff

v.

KEVIN PETERS,
   Defendant

The Defendant appeared before the Court this date for initial appearance. The Court now determines that an alternative, in-custody arraignment date should be set in the event the Defendant remains incarcerated pending arraignment.

It is therefore the order of the Court that an in-custody arraignment in this matter is set for the

18 day of ___June___ , 2003, at 1:30 pm in the courtroom at the Polk County Jail.

FURTHER ORDER

If the defendant is released from custody prior to the date set above for in-custody arraignment, then arraignment will be held on the _17 day of July_ , 2003, at 8:00 a.m. in room 201, Polk County Courthouse as originally scheduled at the time of initial appearance. The defendant is hereby ordered to appear at said time and place. A failure to appear will result in the issuance of a warrant for the defendant's arrest.

He didn't really like the phrase "in the event the Defendant remains incarcerated pending arraignment." Surely his lawyer could get him out of jail before then, couldn't he? A half hour later, he was finally called up to a small desk on the other side of the room. He sat down, and the woman on the other side of the table introduced herself as Judy and explained that she was an investigator for the public defender's office.

"An investigator? I thought I was going to talk to my lawyer," Kevin said.

"Oh, no. Not today. I'll get some information from you and then Mr. Williams will be at your next court date to talk to you."

Kevin couldn't believe what he was hearing. "But that's not until next week. I have to sit here in jail for a whole week?"

"Unless you can bond out. I'm sorry, but that's the way it works. If you're convicted you'll get credit for this time, of course." Despite her sympathetic words, she didn't sound very sympathetic. It was hard to feel bad for each individual person when she talked to a hundred criminals every week, all complaining about having to stay in jail. Innocent until proven guilty is a nice concept, but in most people's minds—including many defense attorneys—if you are arrested, you are probably guilty.

"If I'm convicted? Look lady, I know lots of people probably tell you this, but I really am innocent," he protested.

"Okay, I'll make a note in your file and you can talk with Mr. Williams about it." She handed him a business card with the address and phone number for the Polk County Public Defender's Office on it.

"I don't understand. So, if a police officer decides to arrest someone, then they are just stuck in jail for weeks without being able to protest the charges?"

"Well, if you post bond then you'll be released while waiting for your court date. And the police officers didn't put you in jail by themselves. The Des Moines Police Department has filed a preliminary complaint against you which was signed by a county attorney and a judge." She found three pieces of yellow paper in the file on the desk and handed them to Kevin. They were carbon copy sheets, and he noticed each one had the same caption at the top of the page, listing the plaintiff and defendant, as the order he had just received a couple minutes earlier. On the first page, below the caption it said:

> Defendant is accused of the crime(s) of __Armed Robbery_ in violation of Iowa Code Section(s) 256.3(c) , in that defendant on the _7 day of _June, 20_03, in Polk County, Iowa, unlawfully and willfully _ took $1,200,000 from the Midland Savings and Loan without permission, and used a pistol to accomplish such __.

Below that, he saw several signatures, followed by a section stating:

> THE COURT FINDS PROBABLE CAUSE exists to detain the defendant for the charge(s) set forth above and he/she is to be admitted to bail in the amount of $200,000 .

The next two pages were the same as the first, but charged him with thirty-one counts of false imprisonment and interference with official acts for what the officer described as "attempted to flee during the booking process, refused to comply with officers' orders, and had to be assisted to the ground."

Assisted to the ground? Kevin thought. *That's a bit of an understatement.* He reached up to feel the knot on the back of his head where it had hit the floor the day before.

The investigator showed Kevin where all three complaints were signed by a judge, asserting that probable cause existed for his detainment. Altogether his bond was a whopping $200,000. Judy explained that even if he used a bondsman, he would still have to post $20,000, which he would not get back. He couldn't afford anywhere near that much.

Defeated, Kevin handed the papers back to Judy and returned to his seat along the wall.

CHAPTER 15

Friday, June 13, 3:30 p.m.

"Polk County Public Defender's office. How may I direct your call?"

"Yes, Darren Williams please," Peters said into the dirty payphone provided for the inmates use.

"Let me check if he's here. Can you hold for a minute?"

"Sure," Peters said. He certainly wasn't going anywhere soon.

"Yes, he's here. I'll transfer you," the secretary said after a brief silence.

"Darren Williams here," came a gruff voice from the receiver.

"Yes, hi, Mr. Williams. This is Kevin Peters. I'm a new client of yours, and I wanted to speak with you about my case."

"Peters? I don't recognize the name."

"Yes, well, the judge just appointed you this morning… over here at the jail?"

"Oh, okay. Well, I won't have your file yet then, so I'm not sure there's much I can do at this time. We'll get a chance to…"

"Yeah, here's the thing though; I didn't do it. I shouldn't be in here. You gotta get me outta jail." Peters thought he sounded a little desperate, but then again, he was a little desperate.

"Well, if that's true, then I'm sure we'll be able to get you out soon. What did you say you were charged with?"

Peters hesitated, not wanting to admit it. "Armed robbery."

"Oh. I see… And what's your bond?"

"200 grand."

"200? That seems a little steep. Do you have other charges as well?"

"Yeah, false imprisonment, I think."

"Oh, right." Suddenly a light bulb went off in Williams's head. "You're the guy from that Midland Savings & Loan robbery."

"Right, but I didn't do it. They've got the wrong guy."

"Okay, well at this point, there's not a lot we can do. Until we can get a copy of the minutes, we won't know what evidence they have against you for sure, and even then…"

"Minutes? What minutes?"

"Nevermind. The main thing is that for right now, you'll just have to sit tight. I'll see what I can do about getting your bond lowered, and we'll push the county attorney to file their paperwork soon so we can see what we're dealing with here."

Darren was hoping this would satisfy his client. In reality, there wasn't much he could do to get the bond lowered. He could try to argue with a judge, but that probably wouldn't get him anywhere. People who committed armed robbery generally weren't allowed out in public.

"Okay, well, it sounds like you know what you're doing. I need to get out of here soon though. If I'm in jail for too long, I'm gonna lose my job."

"Yes, I understand." *You job is the least of your problems*, Williams thought. "I'll see what I can do for you. We'll talk again soon."

"Okay, you know where I'll be," Peters said, trying to make a joke. Darren didn't laugh.

"Alright. Talk to you soon, Mr. Peters."

As Peters was escorted back to his cell, he felt once again that they had skipped the "innocent until" part and jumped straight to "proven guilty."

CHAPTER 16

Sunday, June 15, 1:00 p.m.

J enny Peters experienced a little déjà vu as she walked back into the Polk County Jail. Kevin had called and asked her to visit, since he had now added her name to his visitor list. She went through the same routine at the window, giving them her name and her husband's name, except this time they said the visit would be allowed. She waited in the lobby, again studying the sex offender map, until a tall burly deputy came to escort her back to the visiting area.

She followed him down a hall to a small room that reminded Jenny of a school cafeteria. There were several long tables with benches attached on either side, just like there had been at her high school. Her husband sat at one of the tables, wearing a faded gray and white striped jumpsuit. He looked tired and scared, and Jenny realized she was surprised by this. She had told herself this was to be expected but still wasn't prepared. She hesitated for a moment when she saw him, then took a deep breath and forced her legs to continue walking.

"Hi," he said, forcing a small smile. "Thanks for coming. It's good to see you."

"Yeah, of course," she replied, sitting down on the bench opposite him. "How are you?"

"Oh, you know. Could be better," Kevin joked, motioning around him to the building he was trapped in. Jenny just nodded. He noticed that she was leaning back slightly as if trying to keep as much space between them as possible. He wanted to be close to her now; he needed to be close to her, to know that someone was on his side, and he leaned forward on his elbows with his hands reaching across the table.

"They gave me this public defender, but I dunno if he's very good. He doesn't seem to believe that I'm innocent."

"Well, can't you ask them to appoint someone else?"

"I don't think so... I'm not sure. I was hoping maybe you could try to find someone for me."

"You mean hire your own lawyer?"

Kevin hesitated and sat up a little straighter, returning his hands to his lap, "Well... I just don't know what else to do."

"Kevin, I just don't think we can afford it." He recognized her tone and knew she had already made up her mind not to let him pay for a lawyer, which angered him.

"Jen, I didn't do this. Don't you believe me?" he snapped. He couldn't understand why everyone thought he was guilty. Of all people, he thought for sure his wife would be on his side.

"Of course I do..." she said, realizing what he was thinking. "No, it's not that. It's just... like you said before; they'll give up on you when they can't find any real evidence."

"Jen, that's why I'm in here. My attorney says they do have some evidence."

"Well, if you didn't do it, then how could they have any evidence?" she asked, sounding a little more accusatory than she had meant to. He started to argue, and then decided that would get him nowhere and instead offered a compromise.

"Look, how 'bout this. I've got an arraignment on Wednesday. I talked to my lawyer and he said the county has to show us their evidence then. We'll wait and see what happens. If it still looks bad after that, we'll look into how much a real lawyer would cost. Okay?"

Jenny nodded slowly. "Okay, we'll talk about it again later in the week then."

"Okay. So how's everything at home?" he asked, changing the subject.

"Fine. I'm still cleaning up from the other day."

"Why? What happened?"

"They searched our whole house," she explained, "and they didn't put things back."

"I'm sorry," he said quietly.

"It's alright," she replied, and then smiled encouragingly. "It's not your fault. You didn't cause any of this." She sounded confident in her statement, and Kevin thought she believed it. Perhaps he had misjudged her earlier accusations.

"Thanks," he said, genuinely appreciative of the kind words. "I'm sorry if I'm being grouchy. I'm just tired; it's hard to sleep in this place."

"It's okay, don't worry about it."

Kevin shook his head, "I just don't know how long I can stand it. It's awful."

"Yeah, I bet..." She looked down at her hands, and Kevin thought he saw shame on her face. He suspected that she felt bad about doubting him before, or maybe she just felt sorry for him. Either way, he didn't like seeing his wife in pain.

"Hey, it's gonna be okay," he said, trying to reassure her. "I'll be out of here before you know it." He smiled encouragingly, and she nodded even though she knew he wouldn't be. They spent the rest of their time together discussing family and the weather until finally a guard came and informed them their visit was over. Jenny left silently, without hugs, kisses, or even a hand squeeze, and Kevin felt more alone than before she had arrived.

CHAPTER 17

Wednesday, June 18, 3:45 p.m.

Riley and Weathers sat in the office finishing some paperwork on a homeless man they had arrested after lunch. He had been standing at the taxi stand outside the downtown bars, yelling at passing motorists. When Weathers confronted him and told him he needed to leave or he would be arrested, the man had gotten upset. He punched a sign standing next to him, which was on a tall plastic pole. The pole bent backward and then snapped back forward, hitting Weathers in the right ear and making a small cut on the lobe. That was how the man had found himself arrested for public intoxication and assault on a police officer. At least he would have a warm place to sleep for the night.

Weathers's phone rang, and he lazily picked up the handset. Halfway to his head he remembered the cut and switched to his left ear. "Hello?"

"What kind of sloppy investigative work are you guys doing over there?" a voice demanded without introduction.

The attack caught Weathers off guard, and he sat up quickly in his chair. "Um… I'm not sure." He glanced sideways at Riley with a confused look on his face. Riley stopped typing so he could listen in. "Who is this?" Weathers asked, not recognizing the voice.

"This is Ralph Cummings over at the county attorney's office. I'm handling the Peters case."

"Yes, Ralph. What seems to be the problem?"

"The problem is that we arraigned Peters today, and then I received evidence from you this afternoon that was supposed to help make my case."

"Yeah… the tape from Wells Fargo. I sent it over last night," Weathers said, quickly scanning his desk to make sure he had in fact sent it.

"Did you watch it?" Ralph asked.

"No," Weathers replied. Since they had already handed off the case to the attorneys, he had not wanted to waste time going over their evidence for them. "I figured you'd want it as soon as possible. Why? What's on it?"

"Not Kevin Peters."

"What do you mean?" Weathers frowned. He snapped his fingers and waved for Riley to come over to his desk and listen in. Riley sat on the corner of the desk and leaned his head down next to his partner's as Weathers tipped the phone out so they could both hear.

"I mean there's no Kevin Peters carrying large amounts of money into Wells Fargo. There's no Kevin Peters at all," Ralph said, annoyed.

"How is that possible?" Weathers glanced sideways at Riley who was now frowning too.

"I don't know. Are you sure we got the right guy? This is kind of important, Max."

"Yes, I know, Ralph. It's the right guy."

"Well, what do you know about another hostage—Robert Matthews?"

"Matthews?" Weathers asked, looking to Riley for help. Riley just shrugged. "Not much. We haven't found anything to point us in his direction. All the evidence says Peters did it."

"Well, that may be," Ralph replied impatiently. "But the funny thing is, I'm looking at a video of him walking into Wells Fargo on the afternoon of the robbery."

"You gotta be kidding me," Weathers groaned. "Okay, we'll look into it."

"Please do. I don't want any surprises later on. I know you're about to retire, Max, but some of us still care about solving these cases. How 'bout putting a little effort into it?" Ralph abruptly hung up the phone. Weathers replaced the receiver and looked to Riley for his reaction.

"Robert Matthews?" Riley said, ignoring Ralph's attack at Weathers. "Which one was he?"

"The squirrely guy. Said he just laid on the floor in fear the whole time. I don't think it's him. He was one of the regulars we saw on the deli video, works for a messenger service downtown, but nobody saw him go into the vault. Besides, he doesn't match the descriptions we got. He's only 5'8" at most," Weathers said dismissively.

"They could be working together," Riley offered.

"Maybe," Weathers muttered, lost in thought. Riley could see he was working through something in his head, and they sat in silence for a couple of minutes. Finally, Weathers had an idea. "Do we still have Peters's car in the impound?" he asked.

"Yeah, I think so," Riley said. "Why?"

Weathers shrugged, "Just a hunch."

Riley clicked a couple of buttons and brought up the database on Weathers's computer. He pointed at the screen. "Yup, it's right here. Red Pontiac Vibe registered to Kevin Peters."

"I'm gonna go take a look at it. Why don't you have the guys downstairs look into Matthews's finances, and then go over the witness statements again. See if we missed anything."

"Okay. We'll meet back here in an hour?" Riley suggested, checking his watch.

"Sounds good." Weathers walked out of the room and turned left down the hall. As he rounded a corner, Captain Andrews was coming out of a meeting and spotted him.

"Max! Good work on that Midland robbery. I hear they got him arraigned today, and he wants a trial?" Andrews shook his head. "Poor guy doesn't have a chance."

Weathers hesitated, "Uh… yeah. Well, you never know." He side stepped the boss and continued down the hallway. "I was just going to double check our evidence on that case, actually."

Andrews frowned. "Why? Is there something wrong?" he called after him.

"I'm gonna have to get back to you on that one, Captain," Weathers said over his shoulder as he disappeared down a flight of stairs.

When Weathers got to the impound lot, he asked the portly attendant to show him where the Vibe was. The car was unlocked for him, and he climbed into the driver's seat. It was just as he suspected. Weathers was about 6'1", not much taller than Peters, but he had a hard time getting his knees under the steering wheel. Someone else could have driven the car since the robbery, but the wife had said the battery was dead, that it would not start. He leaned forward and inspected the ignition; it seemed fine as far as he could tell. He climbed back out of the car and asked the attendant to get him a screwdriver. The man scurried off back to the building.

Riley dialed Greg's extension. It rang several times and finally Greg's voicemail picked up. He left him a message to check out Robert Matthews as a possible accomplice on the Midland robbery and to get back to him when he had the information on his bank accounts.

Riley opened a drawer and pulled out his notepad. He started skimming through the hostages' statements from the day of the robbery, looking for any information about Matthews. As he flipped through page after page of notes, he realized that no one had mentioned him. Not one person said they had seen him in the bank before the robbery, and most of the hostages could not remember who was where during the incident.

How did we miss this before? he asked himself. But of course, they had been focused on figuring out who was in the vault, not who was not in the lobby, and they had decided on the electrician almost from the start. It had blinded them to other possibilities. With the blinders off now, it seemed so obvious.

Riley turned to his computer and pulled up all of the criminal histories for the hostages. The reports had been scanned into the system with the rest of the case file once they had filed the preliminary complaint and handed the case off to the attorneys. He found Robert Matthews's rap sheet. It was pretty boring—a couple speeding tickets and a petty theft when he was eighteen—except for two charges of carrying weapons. They were both Des Moines cases, so he pulled up the reports for them on his computer. A quick scan through the reports showed that he was arrested both times with a .38 revolver. The gun was apparently licensed to him, but he did not have a permit to carry. Had they done a search on firearms registered to hostages? He was pretty sure Weathers had done that. He would have to check with him when he came back from the impound.

When the attendant returned with the screwdriver, he saw Weathers's legs hanging out the driver's door. He was sitting on an overturned bucket that he had placed on the ground just outside the door as a make-shift seat. As he got closer, he could see that Weathers was lying on his back under the dashboard looking up at the panel under the steering wheel.

"I wasn't sure if it was phillips or regular, so I brought both," the attendant said.

"Phillips."

The attendant handed him the screwdriver, and Weathers began to remove the panel's screws. Once he had the panel off, he could see all the wires running to the ignition.

"Son of a bitch!" he exclaimed.

"What's wrong?" asked the attendant.

"Someone has cut some of these wires and spliced them together."

"You mean they hotwired it?"

"Yup, it certainly looks that way." Weathers was shaking his head as he crawled out of the car. "We didn't see it before because they replaced the panel on the steering column, and we had no reason to take it off and look underneath."

"So... is that important?" the attendant asked. He had thought this car was related to that bank robbery case, not a vehicle theft.

"Yeah, I think it is." Weathers handed the screwdriver to the attendant as he walked back to the building, leaving the car's steering column still torn apart. "Thanks for your help."

"No problem."

Back inside, Weathers and Riley shared their findings with each other. Riley was shaking his head in disbelief, "So, were they working together?"

"I don't think so. If they were in it together, why would he have hotwired the car?"

"Good point. So you think it was a setup then?"

Now Weathers was shaking his head too, "I don't know… It looks that way."

"Peters did steal his fiancé from him." Riley offered. Going back over his notes, he had discovered the forgotten bit of information that gave Matthews a motive. When presented with pictures of other hostages, Matthews had spit on the image of Peters and made several less than endearing comments about the husband of his ex-girlfriend. Weathers had forgotten too.

"Oh yeah, that's right," he nodded. "Well, that's a pretty good reason to frame him."

Riley still wasn't convinced. "What about the money? We know Peters had the fake batteries. Are you saying he didn't use them to get the cash out of the bank?"

Weathers considered this for a minute. "Maybe Matthews switched the batteries. Peters didn't know they were fakes filled with money and carried them out for him."

Riley nodded and added, "And that way if we had found the money it still would have been pinned on Peters." It all made sense now. All of their evidence against

Peters had been so easy to gather because someone had designed it that way.

In Captain Andrews's office once again, Weathers relayed the new development. "Matthews wanted it to be easy to find. He swapped the batteries so Peters would carry the money out for him. Then he flipped the breakers for the cameras, not realizing they weren't recording. During the robbery, he took Peters into the vault with him and probably planted the fingerprint. He stole the Vibe, drove out to Windsor Heights and ran a red light, knowing he would be captured on the camera, then deposited the money into an account in Peters's name. The only thing he hadn't counted on was the camera at Wells Fargo. It all fits."

Andrews was sitting behind his desk, eyes closed, rubbing his temples. "Just yesterday 'it all fit' for Peters. Now you say it all fits for Matthews, and that he framed Peters? Guys, we've got to be sure that we have the right person this time. We can't be arresting a different suspect every week, it looks bad."

"Okay," Riley said. "So, we'll pick up Matthews and see what he has to say. We don't have to drop the charges on Peters until we're sure."

Andrews sighed. "Alright, pick him up. But let's keep this under wraps for now. I don't want word getting out that we can't decide on a suspect."

CHAPTER 18

Thursday, June 19, 1:00 p.m.

"So, Bob. How's the messenger business?" Weathers asked. He was standing in the corner of the interrogation room sizing up their new suspect.

"It's okay, I guess." Robbie was sitting at the same table where they had questioned Kevin just a week earlier.

"Okay?" Riley laughed. "It looks like more than okay." Motioning to a television sitting at the end of the table, he pushed the play button on the remote, and the video from the Wells Fargo lobby appeared on the screen. Robbie watched himself enter through the automatic doors carrying a small bag. He walked across the lobby and up to one of the tellers waiting at the counter. It was hard to see from the angle of the camera, but some papers were handed back and forth, and then Robbie walked back across the lobby and out the doors again.

"I don't understand," Robbie said. "What's the problem?"

"The problem," Riley said, leaning forward with his hands flat on the table, "is that you deposited a million dollars into an account at this bank just three hours after the Midland Savings and Loan was robbed for... how much was it, Max?" he glanced over his shoulder to where his partner had taken up his familiar perch in the corner.

"What is $1.2 million, Alex?" Weathers chimed in as if he were on a game show.

Riley looked back to Robbie. "Wow, what a coincidence. Isn't that an amazing coincidence, Bob?" Robbie just stared at them. He opened his mouth as if to say something, but no words came out.

"Speechless, Bob?" Riley continued. "Let me help you out. You deliver packages all around town, including regular trips to the Midland Savings and Loan. You make what, nine, maybe ten dollars an hour? So you figure, 'I know, I'll rob the bank. I'm there all the time; I know how things work. It'd be easy.' As you plan your heist, you realize you need someone to frame, to make sure you aren't a suspect. One day you make your usual trip to the bank and who do you see? It's the husband of that girl that dumped you. She said she was gonna marry you, and then she left you for him. What a perfect scapegoat! How am I doin' so far?"

Robbie looked up at Weathers, still leaning in the corner, and then back to Riley as if he thought they might be joking. "This video is worthless. I had every reason to be at that bank. I was doing my job. I drop off and pick things up at lots of places around town. You got nothin' on me."

Riley nodded. "I see, so the robber hired you to make the deposit for him? When did this happen exactly? The deposit was made less than an hour after we released everyone from the police station," Riley argued. Robbie just shrugged, either unable or unwilling to give an explanation.

"Well, just to be sure, I called your boss over at Don's Delivery. You did indeed have a delivery to make over at Wells Fargo, for a Jackie Smith," Riley said, consulting his notes. "The problem is, that package was dropped off the night before the robbery, so it obviously couldn't have been the money." Robbie just sat silently, sulking.

"You own a .38 revolver, just like the one used that morning," Weathers offered.

"Oh, so you found the weapon from the bank, did you?" Robbie smiled. "I heard it was still missing."

"Not yet, but we will. We have men searching your house right now."

"Well, if you find it, let me know. I lost that thing years ago."

"Yeah, I bet you did. We've never heard that one before," Riley said, rolling his eyes.

"Look." Robbie leaned back in his chair confidently. "If you've got such a good case, why are we still talking? Why haven't you arrested me yet?"

"Honestly? We've got the arrest warrant signed and they're ready to book you," Weathers lied. "The Captain just wanted to give the rookie here a chance at interrogating a suspect." Robbie looked from Weathers to Riley, trying to determine if this was true.

Riley added, "We've already got enough to convict you. I just figured if I could get you to confess, we wouldn't have to worry about a trial."

Robbie's confidence was quickly fading. "I think maybe I should talk to a lawyer."

"Alright," Weathers said. "We'll see what we can do about that." The officers left the room, shutting Robbie in behind them.

Once outside in the hallway, Riley turned to Weathers. "Now what do we do?"

"We gotta let him go."

"It just doesn't feel right."

"I know. We'll see what they found in the search. If they have the gun, we'll arrest him. Otherwise, we don't have anything for sure yet. Captain won't let us arrest him until we know for sure."

"What about Peters?"

Weathers shrugged. "What about him?"

"You wanna leave him in jail when we think he might be innocent?"

"Who said anything about him being innocent?"

Riley rolled his eyes, "Oh yeah, right. Just 'cause you know someone isn't guilty, that doesn't mean they're innocent. Whatever. You get rid of Matthews then." He stormed off down the hallway, obviously frustrated with his partner. Weathers opened the door to the interrogation room. Robbie was staring at the wall and nervously tapping his fingers on the table.

"Looks like it's your lucky day," Weathers announced. Robbie stopped tapping and looked cautiously at his captor.

"Why's that?"

"We can't get ahold of anyone at the public defender's office, so we're going to give you the benefit of the doubt at this point. But stay in town; we might want to talk to you again."

Robbie was confused. "So… I'm free to go?"

"For now."

Is Kevin Peters Innocent?

Police questioned a new suspect today in connection with the Midland Savings and Loan robbery. No details are being released at this time, but it appears that public pressure may have pushed law enforcement officials into making a premature arrest.

John Claussen, president of the Iowa chapter of the National Innocence Association (NIA), says that each year, thousands of innocent people are arrested and detained for crimes they did not commit. It is a problem that his group is working to correct, and they are quickly adding to their statistics.

The NIA is currently bringing a lawsuit against the state of Iowa on behalf of Matthew Johnston, the accused child molester who was released last week after spending three weeks in jail. An investigation revealed that the accuser's father forged love notes in order to set up his neighbor whom he suspected was having an affair with his wife.

CHAPTER 19

Monday, June 23, 10:00 a.m.

G reg Hughes, the resident computer expert at the Des Moines Police Department, was excited because he had a new computer to search. Officers had brought in a Dell laptop the day before, after it was seized in a search of Robert Matthews's house. As always, Greg started by duplicating the hard drive. This allowed him to investigate without altering the original evidence. It had taken most of the night for his hard drive duplicator to make an exact copy bit by bit, and now he was ready to start snooping.

He attached the copied drive to his test computer and pressed the power button. It booted up into Windows XP. Greg was, of course, quite familiar with this operating system, and it didn't take him long to skim through the personal folders. At first glance, he didn't notice anything useful; nothing related to a bank robbery anyway.

As he perused the program files, he found a folder labeled "Yahoo Mail Toolbar", which indicated that a Yahoo e-mail account had most likely been used on that computer. In the folder were several cookies—small pieces of text that contain data used by websites. One of them included the username for an account: BobMatt88@yahoo.com. It didn't take a degree in computer science to translate "BobMatt" to Robert Matthews.

He searched the temporary internet files for any e-mails that the account holder may have sent or received but found none. This didn't seem to make sense to Greg, which set off red flags. Computers are fairly predictable; after all, they are programmed to process input and spit out a result. Put in A, and out comes B. Put in C, it says D. If A is input and results in D, it's probably because someone changed the programming. People did not usually access an e-mail account and not read or send any e-mails, so Greg knew something was up.

He filled out a subpoena for any and all e-mails relating to username BobMatt88 and faxed it to the Yahoo legal department. He had dealt with them before, as well as most other e-mail services, and they were all very cooperative when served with a subpoena. Greg was always warning people, "If you don't want anyone to know about it, don't write it down. Everything is saved somewhere." E-mails, internet searches, text messages—they were all retrievable later on.

He spent another forty-five minutes sifting through the hard drive's directories but found nothing. Satisfied with his search of the computer, he moved on to Matthews's cell phone while he waited for a response from Yahoo.

Around 1:00 p.m., Riley was finally sitting down to eat a sandwich at his desk when Greg burst through the door waving papers in the air triumphantly.

"Here it is," he announced.

"What?" Riley asked, the sandwich halfway to his mouth.

"Evidence. What else would someone be carrying around in a police station?" Greg laughed.

"Okay. What'd you find?"

"E-mails sent to and from an account opened by Matthews on his home computer."

159

"Let me see," Riley said, no longer interested in the sandwich. Greg began to spread the e-mails on Riley's desk. He pointed at one, indicating that Riley should start with it. Riley picked it up and read:

> **From:** head.hancho@yahoo.com
> **To:** bobmatt88@yahoo.com
> **Subject:** Job Opportunity
>
> Bob Matt –
>
> A mutual friend indicated you might be interested in a job I have that requires a certain level of expertise. Pay is very good. Let me know if you might be available.
>
> - Head Hancho

Before Riley could say anything, Greg was handing him more pages.

> **From:** bobmatt88@yahoo.com
> **To:** head.hancho@yahoo.com
> **Subject:** Re: Job Opportunity
>
> Mr. Hancho,

My friend told me I'd be hearing from you. What'd you have in mind, and how much does it pay?

Your friend,
Bob

From: head.hancho@yahoo.com
To: bobmatt88@yahoo.com
Subject: Re: Job Opportunity

Bob –

How does 200 sound?

I was thinking mid-land, I know the area and it should be simple enough with a Trojan horse.

- Head

From: bobmatt88@yahoo.com
To: head.hancho@yahoo.com
Subject: Re: Job Opportunity

Mr. Hancho,

I'm in, just tell me when.

From: head.hancho@yahoo.com
To: bobmatt88@yahoo.com
Subject: Re: Job Opportunity

Bob –

Fry at Ne. Check out the location and see if you can find us a goat. Perhaps one you don't like?

- Head

From: bobmatt88@yahoo.com
To: head.hancho@yahoo.com
Subject: Re: Job Opportunity

Mr. Hancho,

Dropped by the work site today and found that goat you wanted. I think I

have what is necessary to string him
up too. Looks like everything is ready
for the grand opening.

See you then.

Bob

Riley could not believe what he was reading.
"Well, it's sort of in code, but I think it's clear enough that
he was hired to rob the bank. It all makes sense."

"But what's with the goat?" a voice said from over
Riley's shoulder. He turned and saw that Weathers had
been reading the e-mails from behind him.

"Scapegoat, I assume," Riley shrugged. "He was
telling Bob, Robbie, to find someone to frame."

"Oh, right… But what about the Trojan horse
and the 'fry at Ne'? Some sort of internet slang?"

Riley shrugged. "Perhaps the Trojan horse is
referring to the method of escaping the bank undetected?
Pretending to be a hostage, and slipping out with all the
good guys. Sort of a Trojan horse in reverse, I suppose."

"Oh, of course. That makes sense," Weathers said.
"What about the 'fry at Ne'?" Riley was stumped and
looked to Greg for help, but he just threw his hands up
defensively.

"Hey, I just get the info. I don't interpret it."

Riley shrugged. "We can worry about that later. So, these e-mails were sent from Robert Matthews's computer?"

"Not exactly," Greg replied.

Weathers had been staring at the e-mails again, trying to decipher them and looked up suddenly at Greg, obviously surprised. "So, then how do we know he sent them?"

"Well, Robert's IP address was used to create the e-mail account, but the messages were actually sent and received from a different location."

"Where?"

"Bits and Bites. It's an internet café downtown."

"So, then anyone could have sent those e-mails," protested Weathers.

"No, not true. The account is password protected, so only the owner would be able to access it, unless he gave his password to someone."

"He's right," Riley said. "Matthews probably stopped in the café while making deliveries and did his e-mailing."

Weathers nodded slightly. "So, Greg, do we know who this 'Head Hancho' character is?"

"Nope, sorry. Haven't got that one yet. He was smarter. I'm still tracking down the IP address. But as soon as I know, you'll know."

"Alright, good. Well at least we've got Matthews now."

"So, is that enough to make an arrest?" Greg asked.

"Well, that's up to a judge," Weathers responded, "but I think it will be. Good work, Hughes. Thanks."

"Not a problem," Greg said, bowing slightly. "I am but a humble public servant doing my best to further the greater good of society."

"Yeah, right," Riley replied. "You, along with fifty million other kids, got a degree in computer science and now competition is fierce, and you can't get a job doing anything but data entry, so you work here."

"Can't it be both?" Greg asked with a shrug. Riley and Weathers stacked up the e-mails and headed for the door.

"Good luck with the warrant," Greg called after them as they disappeared around a corner.

CHAPTER 20

Tuesday, June 24, 9:00 a.m.

Weathers walked up to the table and sat on the edge next to Robbie's chair. "Okay, here's the deal. We know this wasn't your idea, and we want to give you a chance to make this a little easier on yourself."

"And why would you do that?" Darren Williams was sitting at the table next to Robbie. A judge had appointed him to represent Robbie, and Darren thought it was quite strange that he was now representing two men accused of committing the same crime, but not as co-defendants. At least he knew he would win one of the cases—obviously one of them was innocent—and it gave him a good defense for the other. If the police couldn't even decide who had committed the crime, how were twelve ordinary people supposed to agree beyond a reasonable doubt?

"One of our computer guys did some checking on your home computer and uncovered an e-mail address that you've been using," Riley explained. "Now, you were smart. You sent and received your e-mails at the internet café on Locust Street downtown, so we couldn't trace it to you. However, you opened the account initially at home. We matched it to your IP address, so we know it's yours."

"I've never been to any internet café," Robbie protested.

Riley pushed a couple pieces of paper across the table in front of them. "These are a series of e-mails provided by Yahoo mail service." Robbie leaned forward to look at them. Riley continued, "In case you've forgotten, I'll refresh your memory." He pointed at one of the pieces of paper. "This first one is where someone named 'Head Honcho', very original by the way, tells you that you need to find someone to frame so the two of you don't get caught." Riley jabbed the second one. "And this is your response back the next day, saying you saw your ex-wife's new husband working at the bank and he'd be perfect."

Robbie looked up from the papers and said, "I've never seen these before. You probably made them up."

"Yeah, probably," Riley rolled his eyes. "But it was enough for a judge to sign an arrest warrant. The judge let Peters out ROR, and we'll most likely be dismissing his case soon." Williams couldn't help but smile a little bit. "Dismiss" was his favorite word, and he rarely heard it from the lips of law enforcement.

"Good for him," Robbie said with disgust.

"You, on the other hand, are going to have a bond of $250,000. We added a malicious prosecution charge to your list. So here's the deal: give us the name of your friend, Mr. Head Hancho, and maybe you'll get out of prison some day."

"Don't say anything," Williams said. "Their case has way too many holes in it. They can't prove where these e-mails came from. We'll never make it to trial."

"I think I'll take my chances with a jury, thanks," Robbie said.

"Okay, have it your way." They handcuffed Robbie and led him down the hall to change into his jail clothes.

As Darren walked to his car, he saw Peters exiting out the side door from the jail. He doubled back and crossed the street to talk to him.

"Kevin, congratulations," he called.

"Uh, yeah. Thanks." Peters was surprised to see him. He had not talked to his attorney since the day of his initial appearance.

"I told you we'd get you out of here," Williams said, as if he had been working all week and had finally succeeded. In fact, he had far too many cases to spend time trying to get a bond reduced, but that was not going to prevent him from taking the credit.

"Yeah, thanks. I appreciate your help," Kevin said, mostly because he thought it was what he was supposed to say. "So, are they dropping the charges then, or what?"

"Well, not officially yet, but they're going to. They've arrested another suspect." Darren nodded toward the jail where Matthews was being booked.

"So, then why haven't they dropped the charges on me yet?" Peters did not understand how they could charge two different people with the same crime.

"Well, they just want to make sure they've got it right this time. But don't worry; they've got more evidence against the other guy than they do against you." Darren set his hand on Kevin's shoulder as if they were old buddies.

"Okay, that's good." Peters was not quite as happy about the situation as his lawyer. Although he was glad to be out of jail, he was still upset about having spent nearly two weeks behind bars for a crime he didn't commit. Darren noticed there was no car waiting to pick Peters up.

"Do you have someone coming to get you?"

"No. I tried to call Jen, but she isn't answering. I didn't even know I was getting out until about an hour ago."

"You need a ride?" Darren offered.

"Nah, I'll be fine. I think I'm going to stop by work and see if I still have a job. It's just a mile from here. I'll walk. Thanks though."

"No problem. Let me know if you need anything else." They shook hands and went their separate ways.

Kevin strolled north along Sixth Avenue with a new appreciation for the outdoors. After twelve days in jail, fresh air was what he missed most. It was a warm summer day, but the tall buildings were funneling a cool breeze through the downtown streets, and he took his time walking and enjoying the city. A small big city with a little over 500,000 people in the entire metropolitan area, Des Moines barely made the list of the top 100 most populous in the country. Still, the insurance based economy had supported some decent sized buildings, including the 630 feet tall "Principal Building" and seven others over 300 feet, and Kevin was finding a new appreciation for the city's beautiful skyline.

After a few blocks, he stopped for a slice of pizza. It was about 10 a.m., and the restaurant was just opening, so he was the only customer. He approached the counter and asked for a slice of Meat Lovers to go. As the pimple-faced kid behind the counter punched his order into the computer, he said, "You look familiar. Do I know you?"

"No, I don't think so," Peters replied, pretending to look through his wallet and trying to avoid eye contact.

"Yeah, I'm sure I've seen you somewhere. You been in here before?" he pressed.

"No, never."

The kid squinted his eyes and thought hard. "Yeah, I know what it is. You're the guy that robbed that bank down the street."

"Nope, sorry. You've got the wrong guy."

"No, it was you. I saw your picture in the paper."

"Yeah, well that was a mistake. They've arrested someone else now."

"Oh, I see." He paused, unsure of how to respond. "Well, that's good then... for you that is. So, how long were you in jail?"

"Umm... I'm not sure." Peters stopped to count in his head. He had lost track of time after the first few days. "I guess it was twelve days."

"Man, that sucks."

"Yeah." Peters was waiting for his change and wished the kid would hurry. He didn't really want to talk about it anymore.

"I was in overnight once; pot charge. It sucked. I can't imagine bein' in there for a week, 'specially if you're innocent."

"Yeah, well I am." He was really starting to hate the word 'if'.

"You should sue, dude."

"Uh, yeah, maybe." Peters was caught off guard by the suggestion. He had never considered it before. He always complained about the frivolous lawsuits people seemed to constantly file, and he felt it was a waste of time and resources; but now things were a little different. Now that he was the one who was wronged, a lawsuit didn't seem like such a bad idea.

The kid handed Peters his change and his pizza, and he retreated to the sidewalk outside where he hoped no one else would recognize him. Devouring the pizza, he continued north toward R & T Electric on University Avenue.

As he walked through the front door, his boss, Chris, looked up from his desk and almost jumped out of his chair in surprise.

"Kevin!" he exclaimed. "They let you out?"

"Yeah, turns out I'm not a bank robber after all," Peters replied, smiling.

"I knew you didn't do it. I told everyone that I thought you were innocent," Chris lied. Actually, he had told the other employees that he was not surprised. "I've had my suspicions about him for a while," he had bragged.

"Yeah, thanks Chris. So, when can I get back out to finish the Cedar Rapids job?"

Chris suddenly lost his grin. "Um, about that. They requested a different electrician. After what happened over at the savings and loan, they just didn't feel comfortable with you. We sent Jerry out to finish up last week."

"Oh, okay. Well, I suppose that's understandable. So, then where am I off to this week?" he asked, anxious to get back to work.

Chris hesitated. "Well…"

"Chris, come on, what's the deal? I've been sitting on my hands for two weeks now. I need something to do."

"Look Kevin. You know I love ya. You're a great employee… but you were all over the news. No one wants a criminal hanging around their business."

Peters could not believe what he was hearing. "But I'm not a criminal!" he exclaimed. "They let me go, remember?"

"Yeah, I know, but the damage is already done. Besides…" he trailed off.

"Besides, what?" Peters demanded, shifting his feet into a fighting stance.

"Well, you had a bond of $200,000. We didn't think you'd be getting out for months, maybe years, so we kinda hired a new guy already."

"What!?" now Peters was getting mad. "I've worked for you for ten years. I'm gone for little more than a week and you've replaced me already?"

"I'm sorry Kevin. I wish there was something I could do, but…" he shook his head.

Peters resisted the urge to punch him and said, "Fine, I don't need this job anyway. Thanks for nothin'," and he slammed the front door on his way out.

CHAPTER 21

Friday, June 27, 8:30 a.m.

hen Ralph Cummings came in to work, he noticed a light blinking on his phone that indicated he had a new message and sighed heavily. The day was starting whether he was ready for it or not. He lifted the receiver and hit the voicemail button. After entering his password and navigating through several prompts, he was finally able to hear the message:

"Yeah, hi. This is Scott Winters, at Winters Chevrolet over here in Iowa City. It's probably nothin', but I thought you should know, just in case. I saw the story on the news, about that Midland Bank gettin' robbed? Well, I noticed you had a suspect in custody, uh… Kevin Peters I believe, and I remembered that back in May, about that time, we had an online order for a Corvette, fully stocked, all the options—delivered it to Ankeny. I didn't think much about it at the time, but I went back and checked, and the order was for a Kevin Peterson. Just seemed like a strange coincidence, I guess… so I wanted to let you know. You can give me a call here at the office…"

Ralph cut the message off by hitting the flash button and waited for a dial tone. He quickly typed in the number for Greg Hughes. Greg did not answer, probably avoiding him. He hit flash again and dialed Weathers's cell.

"Hi Ralph. What do you need?" Weathers asked, knowing this was not just a friendly call and probably meant more work for him. He and Riley were transporting an arrestee back to the station after responding to a domestic call. A man had called 911 when he saw a woman banging on the front door of his neighbor's house with a bucket. He told dispatch he thought it was the neighbor's wife but couldn't see for sure. When Weathers and Riley arrived on scene, they discovered that her husband had locked her out, so she had picked up an empty bucket sitting near the garage by the handle and was swinging it into the door and shouting at him. They were pretty sure she was high on meth and arrested her.

"You're not gonna believe the message I just got." Ralph did not sound happy.

Weathers groaned. "Now what?"

"A car dealer out in Iowa City says he filled an online order for a Kevin Peterson back in May. They delivered a fully loaded Corvette to Ankeny. Those things cost way more than an electrician could afford."

"What? You gotta be kiddin' me."

"Nope. Says he saw the story on the news and wanted us to know." There was a long silence as both men struggled to put the pieces together.

"Okay," Weathers said finally. "So, we know Matthews conspired with someone to frame Peters. Maybe they ordered a car in his name. Part of the frame up?"

"Could be…" Ralph said, trailing off. He didn't sound convinced. "I don't know. This whole case has gone from a slam-dunk to a complete train wreck in no time at all. Somethin' doesn't feel right here. Get with your computer guys and see what they found on those e-mails, and maybe they can look into this online car order. We need to nail down these loose ends. I've got a dismissal sitting on my desk, signed and ready to go to the judge on Peters. I'll hold on to it until this afternoon, but if we wait too long we'll have a lawsuit on our hands. See what you can get for me this morning."

"Alright, I'll get back to you around lunch."

"Sounds good. Thanks."

Weathers set the phone down, flipped on the emergency lights, and hit the gas.

Riley turned to him and asked, "What's up?"

"We need to talk to Greg and get this Midland case straightened out once and for all." He filled Riley in on Ralph's troubling voicemail while their passenger in the back seat carried on a conversation with her hand.

After dumping off their arrestee on another officer back at the station, they found Greg in a corner of the basement staring intently at a computer screen, clicking furiously on the mouse.

"Greg," Weathers began. "I need you to check out an online car order…"

Greg threw an open hand into the air to stop them but kept his eyes fixed on the screen. "Don't tell me." He closed his eyes as if in deep thought. "I bet it's an order for a Corvette, purchased from Winters Chevrolet."

Weathers stopped midstride. "Uh…yeah. That's right, actually."

Greg waived his hand dismissively. "Of course it's right. I'm always right."

"Yeah, I bet," Riley said sarcastically.

Greg turned to face the two of them and said in a serious tone, "You know, everyone's name was Greg until they made their first mistake." He exploded in laughter, apparently quite amused by himself. Riley and Weathers exchanged glances.

"This guy's been staring at a computer screen too long," Weathers muttered, just loud enough for Riley to hear.

When Greg's laughing subsided, he looked at Weathers with a smirk and said, "Let me guess. You want me to track the IP address of the person who made the order because you think Matthews did it in Peters's name as part of the frame up. Is that about right?"

"But I'm guessing you've already done that," Weathers replied.

Greg smiled, "Of course I did. But you're not gonna like what I found." The officers just shrugged, so Greg continued. "Well, I've been trying to track down those e-mails to Matthews, and I found out they were sent from a disposable cell phone, which is why it was so hard to trace."

"You can send e-mail from a disposable phone?"

"Sure, prepaid phones with prepaid internet service. They've all got 'em these days."

"Okay. Do you know who owns the phone?"

"Of course I do. It's the same person that placed the order for the car."

"Great!" Riley exclaimed. "That must be our coconspirator. Whose phone is it?"

"Kevin Peters."

"Kevin Peters?" Weathers said, confused. "So, someone stole his phone then, or something?"

"Nope. I triangulated the location the messages were sent from."

"You can do that?" Weathers asked incredulously.

"Sure, it's pretty simple really," Greg shrugged.

"So, where'd the messages come from?"

Greg smiled and leaned back in his chair, enjoying the suspense. "It's Peters's house."

Weathers frowned. "Well, that's not terribly accurate though right? Matthews could have been parked outside his house or something."

"Could have… but I checked. Matthews was at work out in West Des Moines at the time."

"So, his accomplice sent the messages," Weathers offered.

"I think he did," Greg agreed. Riley and Weathers waited for him to expand on this comment. Greg just kept grinning, clearly enjoying the moment.

Finally Weathers prompted him, "Do you have a theory on who the accomplice might be?"

Greg nodded as he leaned forward in his chair and made a tent with his fingers, "I do... I think Peters is the accomplice." He sat silently as Riley and Weathers processed this. Greg could tell they were thoroughly confused and couldn't see what he was trying to say. "Come on. You guys are the detectives. Think about it. What better way to conceal your guilt then to have someone frame you? I've been looking at the e-mails some more, and I don't think Matthews knew the identity of our mystery accomplice." They didn't respond, and he continued to lay out his case for them.

"The accomplice contacted Matthews first and proposed the idea to him. Then later he suggests the possibility of framing someone, the 'goat', and says, 'perhaps one you don't like.' Peters knew when Matthews saw him at the bank he'd jump at the chance to frame the person who stole his girl." Weathers didn't want to admit it, but Greg was making sense.

"So, Peters hires someone to rob the bank, and then has that person frame him? That's crazy," Riley said.

"Crazy enough to be the truth," Weathers said. He turned to Greg. "Are we sure about this? You've got the documentation, everything we need to convince a jury?"

"It's pretty solid. Like I said, I'm never wrong."

"No," Weathers corrected, "you said you're always right." He smiled and left the room, punching Ralph's number into his phone.

FRAMED, maybe?

Police flip-flop again
on Midland Robbery

It has been two weeks since police first arrested Kevin Peters for the armed robbery of the Midland Savings and Loan. He was subsequently released from the Polk County Jail after serving twelve days for a crime it seemed he did not commit. Now, investigators again believe he may have been involved after all.

Polk County Attorneys are proceeding with their case against both Peters and codefendant Robert Matthews. E-mail messages sent from Peters to Matthews indicate that they were both in on the plot to relieve the bank of its cash reserves, and that Matthews intentionally set up Peters in an attempt to disguise the fact that they had conspired together.

Prosecutors are in the process of preparing for trial against both men as their attorney, Darren Williams, has indicated that no plea deals will be made, no matter what is offered. In a written statement delivered by their attorney, both men maintained their innocence and called upon the Des Moines Police Department to continue their search for "the true criminals."

National Innocence Association President John Claussen, in town to settle the association's pending lawsuit against the city, commented that "it is a sad day for the wrongfully accused. If these e-mails show what they are reported to, Kevin Peters and Robert Matthews's actions have only continued to hinder the public's perception of people who truly are victims of a frame up."

CHAPTER 22

Tuesday, November 18, 11:00 a.m.

"Is the prosecution ready for its opening statement?" Judge Matthes asked. She had left the jail a couple weeks earlier when the district court judges did their semi-annual rotation. Working back at the courthouse again, she was now in the pool of potential trial judges and had drawn the infamous Midland Robbery.

"Yes, Judge," Ralph said from the table in the center of the courtroom. He stood, consulting a yellow legal pad, and turned to face the jury. Working from his notes, he attempted to simplify their case as much as possible. "Ladies and gentlemen of the jury, you have been called here today to decide the guilt of these two men." He turned and held his hand out, motioning to the defendants.

"As you hear testimony from several witnesses explaining the complexities of the events leading up to armed robbery and kidnapping, remember that it all boils down to one simple fact—Kevin Peters and Robert Matthews conspired to hold thirty men, women, and children against their will, nearly killing one of them, so that they could abscond with more than a million dollars from hard-working Iowans like yourselves."

He paused for dramatic effect and consulted his notes. "We will show you e-mails between the defendants which document the conspiracy. We will show you video of both defendants visiting the bank several times as they plan the heist. We will also show you video of the defendants depositing the stolen money into an account which was opened in their name. The defense will try to cloud the issue, claiming the evidence is all circumstantial."

He dropped his notepad on the table and fixed his stare on the jurors, conveying as much intensity as possible. "My friends, do not be fooled. Despite what you may have heard on television, circumstantial evidence is strong evidence. Let me offer you an example."

He walked toward the jury box and half sat, half leaned casually against the end of the table. He was just a friendly guy telling an amusing anecdote.

"Let's pretend you just baked a nice, hot, blueberry pie and set it out on the counter to cool. You leave the room to do other things and return a few minutes later to find half of the pie is missing. There are crumbs on the counter and your son sits on the floor with blue streaks around his mouth. Now, you have no direct evidence that he ate the pie. There are no witnesses who saw him eat the pie. He doesn't admit to eating the pie. Yet you conclude 100%, beyond a shadow of a doubt, that he ate the pie."

Ralph paused and noticed several jurors nodding slightly. "I, therefore, submit to you that circumstantial evidence does not translate to weak evidence; it merely requires a reasonable person to connect the dots, something that five-year-olds do in coloring books."

Ralph sat down, feeling he had adequately prepared the jury for what his witnesses were about to present. Now it was Darren Williams's turn. This was not the first time he had represented codefendants, but it wasn't common either. Things were always a little tricky for the attorney if one of his clients wanted to place the blame on the other. So far that hadn't been the case, though. Peters and Matthews had simply denied any knowledge of anything related to the robbery. Darren had, of course, tried to convince his clients to plea and take a deal, but they had refused. Darren argued that the prosecution had several solid pieces of evidence, and they had nothing at all to present in response, but that didn't seem to matter to the two accused.

"Mr. Williams," the judge announced. "You're up."

Darren thanked the judge and then stood and studied the jurors for a moment. He saw that the juror in the front row at the east end of the jury box had disgust on his face. To him, Darren was already the bad guy. He thought back to the jury selection process earlier in the morning. He remembered that this particular juror, Norm Spalinski, had said he worked as a security guard at Valley West Mall. Normally, Darren would have tried to strike him from the jury. In his experience, most security guards were wanna-be cops who didn't make the cut. They generally had an idolized view of the police and naturally took the prosecution's side. However, he also got the impression that Norm was a little slow; he had seemed confused by even the most basic questions. Darren was counting on the complexities of the case to prevent Norm from comprehending the state's argument. As he began his opening, he looked directly at Norm.

"My name is Darren Wiliams, and I will be representing the young men you see sitting next to me today. Despite what Mr. Cummings here would like you to believe, the evidence against my clients is flimsy at best. These dots he wants you to connect are miles apart.

"Have you ever looked up in the sky at night and formed shapes, or constellations, out of the stars? If there are enough dots, you can pick and choose the ones you want to use and make any picture that suits your purposes." He bent down to the table and made some marks on a legal pad. He held the picture up to show the judge, and then the jury, five small circles he had drawn in a sort of t-shape—one in the center with others on either side and above and below the first.

"What do you see?" He scanned their faces, giving them time to think. "Perhaps you see a cross?" he suggested to Mrs. Rohlf, the church secretary in the back row, as he used a pencil to connect the dots with vertical and horizontal lines. Then he turned to Mrs. Corwin, the high school science teacher next to her, "Or maybe it's a plus sign." He glanced around at the others and turned the page forty-five degrees. "If you look at it a little differently it could be an X or a roman numeral ten."

He drew more lines connecting the outside points so it now looked like a square with an X inside. "Any of you bowlers? Maybe it's a strike." He glanced at Norm, who was wearing a Minnesota Twins shirt, and turned the page back upright. He erased the horizontal and vertical lines leaving a diamond with a dot in the center. "Maybe we leave one dot out to make a baseball field." He could see now that he had their attention.

"The point is, ladies and gentlemen, dots are just dots until you connect them. And I don't know about you, but I personally don't know many five-year-olds who can do a 'connect the dots' without the numbers." He tossed the notepad onto the table and pointed at Ralph. "The prosecutor is trying to number the dots in the order that suits him best, but that doesn't make it the truth." He nodded to the judge, indicating he was done, and took his seat next to his clients.

The rest of the morning was spent listening to several of the victims talk about their experience being held hostage by a masked gunman at the Midland Savings and Loan. As expected, none of them could say for sure who was behind the mask. Most just said they were frightened and gave a general description of an average white man with brown hair. After a long morning of repetitive testimony, Judge Matthes announced that they would break for lunch, and Ralph informed her they would be moving on to new material when they returned.

By one o'clock, everyone was back in their places, and Greg was on the witness stand. Ralph began the afternoon by walking him through the steps he had taken to find the e-mails.

"So, how do we know these accounts belong to the defendants?" Ralph asked.

"Well, BobMatt88@yahoo.com was created on Mr. Matthews's home computer, and Head.Hancho@yahoo.com sent his e-mails from a cell phone at Mr. Peters's house."

"Okay, and what did these e-mails reveal?"

Greg consulted a printout of the e-mails that Ralph had entered into evidence a few minutes earlier. As he read the messages, Judge Matthes and the jurors followed along on their own copies.

"From Peters: A mutual friend indicated you might be interested in a job I have that requires a certain level of expertise. Pay is very good. Let me know if you might be available."

"And how did Matthews respond?" Ralph prompted.

"My friend told me I'd be hearing from you. What'd you have in mind, and how much does it pay?"

"Okay, and they start using some sort of code at this point, correct?"

"Yes, that seems..." Greg began, but was interrupted when Darren objected.

"Your honor," argued Darren. "How can this witness possibly know what the author of an e-mail was intending to say? His expertise is in computer forensics, not mind reading."

Judge Matthes shrugged at the prosecution. "I think he has a point there, Ralph."

Ralph knew it was important to explain to the jury what they believed the e-mails meant. He remembered a rumor he had heard about Judge Matthes and her lack of computer knowledge. Supposedly, her court attendant handled all of her e-mails for her because she didn't even know how to turn the thing on. He decided to play to her ignorance.

"Judge, I believe as a computer scientist, Mr. Hughes is certainly qualified to testify as to the content of e-mails and the various shorthand commonly used in online chats. Just as we in the legal profession have a vocabulary not shared by the ordinary citizen, so too does the internet. Not everyone here has a lot of experience with the current lingo, and Mr. Hughes may be able to provide us with some insight. For example, how many people here know what 'lol', 'omg', 'brb', or 'lmao' mean?" The judge simply stared at the back wall of the courtroom, considering the situation. It was clear that she had no idea what the letters Ralph had just mentioned were supposed to mean.

"Um, your honor," Greg said, raising his hand as if he were back in grade school. "If it makes any difference, I did take several code breaking classes in pursuit of my computer science degree." This seemed to seal the deal for the judge, and she nodded her approval.

"Alright. I'll allow it, but be careful. I don't want to hear any speculation."

Ralph smiled and nodded. "Thank you, Your Honor." He then turned back to Greg. "So, Mr. Hughes, you were saying you had to decipher some of the messages?"

"Yes. Well, for the most part they were fairly straightforward, but some of the details were sort of hidden, presumably in case the e-mails were ever discovered after the fact."

"Is this something that is commonly done by people, or would it seem to indicate that the person had something to hide?" Ralph queried.

"Objection," Darren called from his table. "He can't know the intentions of the person who wrote the e-mail."

"Sustained. I told you no speculation."

Ralph paused for a moment to reformulate his approach. "Mr. Hughes, why don't you just read us the sections of the e-mail that you believe are coded and tell us what you, as an expert, believe they mean?" He glanced over his shoulder at Darren to make sure he was okay with this question. Darren glared back at Ralph but made no indications he was objecting.

"Well, there is some talk about 'mid-land' as the location, which clearly could be the Midland Savings and Loan. And then when Matthews asks about the time,

Peters says 'Fry at Ne', which actually had us confused for a while. I couldn't understand why the Ne was capitalized."

Ralph looked down the jury box until he found Mrs. Corwin, the science teacher. He locked eyes and kept her gaze as he asked Greg, "And what did you determine?"

"Well, I did what I always do when I'm stumped. I Googled it. I came up with the stock symbol for Noble Corporation, the abbreviation for Nebraska, and the symbol for the element neon. Stock symbols and states are generally written with both letters capitalized, so the element neon was the most likely answer."

Ralph saw a small smile on Mrs. Corwin's face and knew she had already figured it out. He turned back to Greg. "Neon, Mr. Hughes? I'm afraid you're gonna have to help me out. It's been a while since I took chemistry."

Greg smiled. "It's pretty clever really. Neon is the tenth element. 'Fry at Ne.' In other words 'Friday at ten'."

Ralph feigned surprise. "Friday at ten? Wasn't the Midland Bank held up at ten o'clock on a Friday?"

Greg nodded. "Yes, it sure was." Ralph furrowed his brow as if he were deep in thought, still piecing it together. Of course he already knew all of this, but he felt that it helped him relate to the jurors if it seemed like they were all working it out together. It was almost as if he were climbing over the short wall into the jury box and joining their team.

Darren had few questions on cross-examination other than to reaffirm that Greg was, in fact, not a mind reader, and the e-mails could certainly mean something else entirely. Once Greg had been dismissed by the judge, Officer Jared Riley was called in to testify. Being new to the police force, it was his first time in court for a trial. Ralph had prepped him as much as he could, but Riley still felt a little nervous.

He loosened up some as Ralph walked him through their investigation, having him explain how the case had unfolded, ultimately leading to the arrest of the two defendants. The butterflies came back as Darren was offered a chance at the young officer. Darren wasted no time with small talk and jumped in feet first.

"Officer Riley, do you often break procedure and just do your own thing?"

Riley frowned, apparently caught off guard. "Um, no. I don't understand why..."

Darren did not wait for him to finish. "Well, you are extremely new to the Des Moines Police force, are you not?"

"Yes, but that doesn't mean..."

"So, perhaps it's just inexperience then? Is that the problem?"

"Objection," Ralph practically yelled. "Your honor, this kind of attack is completely unnecessary and unsubstantiated."

Darren jumped in before the judge could say anything. "Judge, if you will just give me a minute, this is going somewhere." Judge Matthes raised her eyebrows and stared down at Darren, silently telling him to hurry up and make his point. When she felt he had gotten the message, she motioned for him to continue.

Riley's frown had turned into a stare, and he was gritting his teeth. "I don't know what you're getting at here, but I know procedure, and I follow it."

"Do you?" Darren prodded.

"Yes," Riley insisted. Darren shrugged and produced a binder from his briefcase. He carried it to the witness box and handed it to Riley. He had Riley hold it up and explain to everyone what it was.

"It appears to be a copy of the Des Moines Police Department procedural guide," Riley explained. He wasn't sure where this was going, but he knew he didn't like it. He looked at Ralph for help, but he was just as confused as his witness.

"Officer Riley, would you please open up the binder to the section on handling media inquiries?" Darren asked. Riley's stomach dropped into his feet. As he turned the pages, he felt like he was dreaming. His arms moved slowly, as if he were swimming. Surely Darren couldn't know about Emma, could he? Riley read aloud the department's policy on not talking to reporters and funneling all inquiries through the media liaison.

"So, as you understand it," Darren continued, "the department's policy is not to talk to reporters... at all."

"That is correct."

"And you have told us that you always follow procedure, so you certainly didn't talk to reporters about the case." Riley didn't respond. He just stared at Darren, trying to light him on fire telepathically. It didn't work.

"Officer Riley, what if I told you that I have a reporter waiting outside this courtroom who is willing to come in and testify that you divulged details about the case throughout the investigation?" Riley wasn't sure what to say and looked at Ralph, pleading for help with his eyes.

Finally Ralph stood up. "Uh... objection, Your Honor... Mr. Williams is..." he paused, not knowing what reason he had to object. Then, after a second, an idea came to him. "The prosecution has not been made aware of this witness, Judge."

Judge Matthes looked over the top of her glasses at Ralph, knowing he was fishing. "Mr. Cummings, if the defense decides to call this witness, you may bring your objection at that time. Right now, he is simply asking *your* witness a simple question." She turned to Riley. "Young man, you'll have to answer."

Riley shifted in his seat and tried to regain his composure. "I may have inadvertently given some information to a reporter early on in the investigation. But I didn't know she..."

"Thank you," Darren interrupted, holding his hand in the air to stop the explanation. "Just answer the question please. So, really you just follow procedure when it suits you, not all the time."

"Is that a question?" Riley shot back.

Darren threw his hand in the air in exasperation and sighed theatrically. "I guess I have no more questions."

Before Darren could sit down, Ralph was out of his seat and making his way forward. "Redirect, Your Honor?" Judge Matthes just waved her hand, motioning for him to proceed.

Ralph walked toward the witness stand until he was far enough past the judge's bench that only the witness could see his face and his back was to the jury box. He mouthed, "You'd better fix this," and then stepped to the side and turned so the jury could see him again.

"Officer Riley, you said, 'But I didn't know she...'. What was it you wanted to tell us?"

"I didn't know she was a reporter. I was out with some friends, and a girl just started talking to me. I didn't give her any details. I just said that I was working the case and that we were close to making an arrest. I didn't even tell her who the suspect was."

"So, in your eyes, you were still following procedure?"

"Yes," Riley said confidently.

"Thank you," Ralph said, returning to his seat.

Knowing Ralph would ask for it, Judge Matthes announced they would be taking a short break, and everyone started to file out into the hall. Ralph grabbed Riley's arm and led him to a corner of the room that was unoccupied.

"What the hell was that all about?" he hissed.

Riley shrugged. "I'm sorry. I didn't think anyone knew about it. I don't understand how he found out."

"The reporter probably told him," Ralph said, a little louder than he intended. He looked around to make sure no one was listening. Riley just nodded, not sure what to say. "Is there anything else I need to know about?" Ralph demanded. Riley thought about the trick they had pulled at Peters's house, and how Emma had threatened to divulge the fourth amendment violation she had witnessed. He considered telling Ralph but decided that if Darren knew about it, he would have brought it up during his ambush on the stand a few minutes earlier.

CHAPTER 23

Tuesday, November 18, 3:45 p.m.

A s Weathers finished up his testimony after the break, Riley sat nervously on a bench outside the courtroom. He knew his partner was no doubt being subjected to the same questions about Riley's mishandling of procedure. During the break, Riley had warned him about the probable attack, not wanting Weathers to cover for him again and allow Darren to discredit both officers.

Weathers had been forced to stay in the hall during Riley's testimony, because witnesses generally weren't allowed in the courtroom until after they testified. That prevented them from changing their statement based on what other witnesses had said.

"How'd the defense attorney find out about her?" Weathers had asked, obviously startled by the turn of events.

"I don't know. Ralph thinks Emma probably told him," Riley said, looking up and down the hall to check for eavesdroppers. Weathers considered this for a moment.

"Do you think she told him about..." Weathers raised his eyebrows as if to say "you know what."

Riley shook his head. "That's what I was worried about too, but I don't think so. I figure if he did know about it, why didn't he bring it up when he had me on the ropes? Or he could have filed a motion to suppress the evidence found at the house before we even went to trial and avoid the whole thing."

Weathers nodded, but didn't seem quite as convinced as Riley. "Well, I guess we'll just see what happens. He might not even bring it up. She was trespassing and interfering with an investigation at the time, and it'd be her word against four police officers." Ralph walked by and motioned for Weathers to follow him into the courtroom. Riley wished him luck and took his spot on the bench.

It had been forty-five minutes, and Riley was still waiting for court to wrap up for the day. The officers' testimonies that afternoon would be the end of Ralph's case, and then Darren would have a chance to present his witnesses, most likely the next morning. The hall was beginning to get more crowded as other courtrooms completed the day's business. Riley saw several other officers he knew leaving hearings or other trials and exchanged greetings with them as they passed. Several reporters had started to loiter nearby, hoping to catch Darren or Ralph as they left for the day. Riley scanned the faces and noticed a familiar one.

"Emma!" he called and waved for her to come over where he was sitting. She hesitated and glanced toward the courtroom, then crossed the hall and sat next to him on the bench.

"Officer Riley, how's it going?" she smiled. He didn't smile back.

"How could you?" he demanded.

"What do you mean?" she frowned, apparently not knowing what he was upset about.

"You know you may have just blown the case for us."

She held up her hands defensively. "Look, I don't know what it is you think I've done, but I'm not trying to hurt your case. Between you and me, I'm hoping those two get locked up for good. If you read my articles, you'd know

I'm usually on the side of law enforcement." He studied her for a minute, trying to decide if she was telling the truth.

"Well, then what were you planning on testifying about?" he challenged.

"Testify? I'm not testifying about anything," she said.

"When I was on the stand earlier, Mr. Williams said he had a reporter who was willing to testify that I gave her information about the case. He's trying to show that I don't follow procedure and cast doubt on the whole investigation."

"Well, I've never even met him before, let alone agreed to testify." Suddenly it hit Riley like a ton of bricks, and his stomach returned to his feet. He leaned forward, resting his face in his hands.

"I'm such an idiot," he groaned.

"What?" she asked, confused by his sudden change of attitude.

"He was bluffing!" Riley exclaimed. "He didn't know that I talked to anyone. He must have heard about the e-mail that went out to the department about people leaking information. He was fishing. He probably assumed it was either Weathers or me, and if I hadn't taken the bait, he would've tried the same thing with him. How could I be so stupid?" Emma just sat next to him on the bench, not sure what to say.

"Maybe it's not as bad as you think," she offered finally. "Your partner has a lot of experience and is a very credible witness." Riley nodded. Hopefully she was right.

Suddenly, the doors opened, and people began filing out of the courtroom. Riley found Ralph and Weathers and told them about his conversation with Emma. Ralph said he thought Weathers had been able to patch the hole and upright the ship. He explained how Darren had started in on the same questions, but Weathers just shrugged it off.

"Yeah, he slipped up and said a few things to a reporter," he had explained. "But he didn't give any details. I've been on the force for over thirty years. I helped write the book, and everything in this investigation was done according to procedure. The case practically solved itself. Why would we need to cheat?"

Riley was only slightly consoled by the repair job his partner had done. They informed him that the defense would be presenting their case in the morning, but that it probably wouldn't last long.

"Who are their witnesses?" Riley asked.

"Just the defendants themselves. They have no one else," Ralph smiled.

CHAPTER 24

Thursday, November 20, 11:15 a.m.

Everyone waited patiently as the jury filed into the room and took their seats in the outdated brown chairs. Ralph looked eagerly for some indication of how they had ruled. Like a poker player reading his opponent, Ralph could often pick up on the little tells from the jury. On this day, the jurors avoided eye contact, which was usually a bad sign. But then again, he didn't see any of them looking at the defendants either. He glanced over at Robbie and Kevin. They both seemed very nervous. "Good," he thought. "They should be worried."

Riley and Weathers were sitting in the back of the room, anxiously awaiting the fruits of their labor. Weathers saw Kevin's wife, Jenny, sitting off to one side, nervously chewing on her fingernails. Kevin's parents were also present, as was Robbie's brother. The rest of the benches were mostly filled with reporters and other attorneys interested in the case. It was not every day that someone in Des Moines, Iowa was tried for armed robbery, and even less often that a person was tried for intentionally having themselves framed for armed robbery.

The defendants had both testified at the start of the day, but neither one had done much to help their cause. They both denied having any involvement in, or knowledge of, the robbery but when presented with the state's evidence, had no explanation. Darren had known their case was weak going into the trial and had pushed for pleas from his clients, but they had both refused to "admit to something they didn't do."

The room became silent as the judge addressed the jury, "Have you reached a unanimous verdict?" Several jurors nodded as the foreman confirmed they had completed their civic duty. Norm was the first juror to steal a glance at the defendants, and his eyes told Ralph everything he needed to know.

Judge Matthes reached for her glass of iced tea and took a long drink before leaning forward toward the microphone, savoring the moment as the entire room waited impatiently. "I will now read the verdict as set forth by the jury as a whole and signed as such by all twelve members." She glanced around the room, just in case someone wasn't listening.

"In the matter of State v. Robert Matthews, on count one of the indictment, the charge of armed robbery, we find the defendant guilty. On counts two through thirty-one, the charges of false imprisonment, we find the defendant guilty on all counts." There were murmurs from the crowd as everyone reacted to the verdict. The rulings were repeated for State v. Kevin Peters—guilty on all counts. "I am ordering that the defendants be held without bond and am setting this matter for sentencing two weeks from today, back here in this courtroom."

The judge finished by notifying the defendants of their right to file a motion for a new trial, but no one was listening at that point. Several of the reporters were already leaving the courtroom, anxious to relay the verdict to their bosses. It would be the lead story on every news channel that night and on the front page of every paper the next morning. Although their sentences were yet to be determined, everyone knew they would be spending many years as guests of the Iowa Department of Corrections.

Peters & Matthews, Guilty

Jury convicts Midland Robbers on all 31 counts

Citizens of Des Moines can rest a little easier now knowing that the men who held dozens of people hostage and stole more than a million dollars are safely behind bars.

Kevin Peters and Robert Matthews were found guilty yesterday in Polk County District Court. The jury spent just over an hour in deliberations and returned a unanimous verdict of guilty to armed robbery and false imprisonment.

Trial judge, Hon. Jean Matthes, has set a sentencing date of December 4th. County attorney Ralph Cummings, stated that they are very pleased with the results and are not worried about their chances should the defense decide to appeal.

The case has been followed quite closely by many in the legal community as the complexities of the conspiracy and apparent frame up caused trouble initially for the police. Local attorney Rick Owens, who was present for the verdict yesterday, commented that this was "one of the most interesting cases we've had in Iowa."

Louis Seegers, a law professor at Drake University, even brought his class to court to watch part of the trial as a learning experience. "I was getting so many questions about the case in class, that I felt it would be a good opportunity for a field trip," he explained.

The unusual case has garnered much media attention, and even some criticism that the department has tried too hard to cover up the details of an apparent

cont on page 4A

EPILOGUE

15 hours before the hostage situation
at the Midland Savings and Loan

As the elderly janitor carried two large bags of trash out the back door of the Midland Savings and Loan, a cute young woman jogged across the parking lot toward him. She had a large commercial battery in each hand and appeared to be struggling with the weight. As she reached the back door, she dropped them on the ground with a thud.

"Hey, sorry I'm late. Any chance I can take these inside?"

"The bank's closed, ma'am. Sorry," he responded. The old man stepped halfway through the door, but the woman slid sideways in front of him, blocking his path to the dumpster.

"Oh, man. My boss is gonna kill me," she whined. "I told him I'd have the new batteries ready for him in the morning. They're for the temporary lighting in the lobby."

"Oh yeah, for the electrician," he said, glancing across the parking lot at a gray truck that said R & T Electric across the side. "Can't you hook them up in the morning?"

"I would, but I gotta chaperone my kid's field trip. They're going to the zoo," she explained. "My ex is fighting me for custody, and I'm trying to show the courts I can be a fit mother. If I lose another job, I don't know what'll happen..." The janitor adjusted the heavy bags in his arms, but the woman stood her ground, not giving him room to pass.

"Well, it won't take long, will it?" he conceded.

"No, I know where they are. I just need to hook these up quick."

"Alright, but be fast. I could get in big trouble letting you in. I can't afford to lose my job either. My wife is fighting cancer, and I need every cent I can scrape together to pay the hospital bills."

"It'll be our little secret. I'll just be a minute. Thanks!" She flashed him a big smile and stepped to the side. He maneuvered the large bags past her, and as he did, she leaned in and gave him a quick peck on the cheek. He was caught off guard and didn't notice as her left hand picked the key ring off his belt clip. She grabbed the batteries and slipped into the bank, the door locking as it closed behind her.

Alone in the bank, Jenny Peters quickly found the vault and ducked inside. On Thursday nights, the vault was left open so the janitor could clean the floors. He would shut and latch the door when he was done later in the evening. She pulled the tops off of the fake batteries and began to remove stacks of counterfeit bills hidden inside where hazardous chemicals would normally have been. They weren't very good counterfeits, but they didn't need to be. It just had to look like the money was there when the manager opened up in the morning. No one would actually use the bills or look at them closely. In fact, only the top bill in each stack even had printing on it, the rest were just green paper.

The batteries were soon filled with stacks of real bills from the shelves at the back of the vault, and the pile of fakes replaced them on the shelves. She heard pounding on the back door and knew she didn't have much time left. She replaced the tops on the fake batteries and dragged them out to the lobby. Running down the hall to the utility room, she found the breakers for the cameras, and flipped them off.

By now the janitor had walked around the building and was approaching the large glass doors in front. He pushed his face up to the glass, peering inside, and saw the woman walking into the lobby from the hallway. She waved to him and smiled, and he motioned for her to open the door. She unlatched the deadbolt and he said, "I thought you just needed to hook up the batteries to the lights in the lobby. What were you doing back there?"

"Oh, I got some grease on my hands, so I slipped into the restroom quick to rinse them off. That's okay, isn't it?" She flashed another smile as she grabbed the two fake batteries full of money sitting in the middle of the lobby and headed out the door. "Thanks for everything. I owe you one." And then she was gone.

The janitor looked around the small lobby, and as far as he could tell everything seemed to be in place. He walked over to the vault and peeked inside. The large stacks of money were still resting safely on the shelves along the back wall. He walked down the hall to the bathroom and saw that the sink was, in fact, wet. On his way to the back door, he found his keys sitting on the floor along the wall. Shaking his head, he continued with his nightly duties, making a mental note to get a stronger belt clip that would hold his keys better.

On her way home from the bank, Jenny stopped by Drake University and met with Toby Brandt in his dorm room. She pulled $200,000 and a .38 revolver out of her purse and set them on his desk. "Make sure everything goes smoothly tomorrow," she said. The next day, Toby would chain shut the doors to the Midland Savings and Loan, shoot the gun in the air, yell at people a little bit, and then enter the vault. While the police waited outside, he would have plenty of time to break into the safety deposit box he had rented a few weeks earlier. The box required two keys—his key and the "guard" key. He of course had his own key but would have to pick the other lock on his box. Once opened, the counterfeit money, the gun, and the mask would all be hidden inside. Then Toby would simply wait for the police to enter the building, and in the ensuing chaos, he could slip into the crowd as a hostage.

"Don't worry. It'll be fine," he reassured her. They said their goodbyes, and he stood in the doorway watching her stroll down the dirty hall, knowing he would probably never see her again. Part of him wished he could go with her, but he knew she would never go for it. Besides, it'd be hard to become a famous actor if he were in hiding.

From the university, Jenny drove to Don's Delivery and dropped off the small bag of money to be delivered to Wells Fargo the next morning. She paid in cash and signed her name as "Jackie Smith". From there,

Jenny hurried home, wanting to arrive before her husband, Kevin, got back from his poker game and noticed she had taken his company truck. As she grabbed a snack in the kitchen, she sent one last message from a disposable cell phone to a dummy e-mail account she had created.

About a month earlier, she had shown up at her old fiancé, Robbie's, door and told him that she and Kevin were having problems and were thinking about going to a marriage counselor. She told him that she didn't know who else to turn to for advice. Robbie invited her into his apartment and offered her something to drink. She asked him for a White Russian, knowing it would take him a few minutes to find and mix the ingredients. While cupboards were searched in the next room, she logged onto the computer resting precariously on a wobbly desk in one corner of the living room and quickly created a yahoo e-mail account that Robbie would never use—BobMatt88@yahoo.com.

In the ensuing weeks, she had sent several messages to and from this account using the disposable phone that had been purchased in her husband's name and a computer at a local internet cafe. No one had read the e-mails, of course, but she was confident they would be found when the police eventually seized Robbie's computer.

Once the last message was sent, she turned the phone off and hid it behind the refrigerator. She would use it again in a week to order a Corvette from a dealer in Iowa City and then toss the phone off the dam into Saylorville Lake.

She changed into her pajamas and returned to the kitchen. Retrieving an empty can of Diet Pepsi from the recycling bin, she placed it on the end table in the living room and reclined on the couch, trying to look like she'd been lounging all night. With all the preparations in place, she turned on the news and settled in to relax and enjoy her last night as a poor woman.